R

Dr Lesley Colman took on the job as locum to a small general practice in Cornwall because she desperately needed the money. She didn't want to work for the infuriating Dr Neil Rodway any more than he wanted her . . .

Having written fiction and non-fiction for children of all ages for many years, Jennifer Eden turned to writing Doctor–Nurse Romances first as a challenge, then with increasing enjoyment as a new creative world opened up for her. She is very lucky in having a good back-up team of a husband and two sons with medical and dental qualifications. Having also experienced the other side of medicine as a patient, she hopes she is able to convey something of that with understanding too.

STOP-GAP DOCTOR

BY

JENNIFER EDEN

MILLS & BOON LIMITED
15–16 BROOK'S MEWS
LONDON W1A 1DR

First published in Great Britain 1985
by Mills & Boon Limited

ISBN 0 263 75323 9

Set in 10 on 11½ pt Linotron Times
03–0286–53,500

Photoset by Rowland Phototypesetting Limited
Bury St Edmunds, Suffolk
Made and printed in Great Britain by
Richard Clay (The Chaucer Press) Limited
Bungay, Suffolk

CHAPTER ONE

THE girl with the ash-blonde hair and serious brown eyes was alone in the hospital corridor at that moment—alone and on edge. If anyone else had been there to see they would have noticed the tense set of her mouth and the agitated way she played with the stethoscope hanging round her neck.

They would also have seen by the name-tab pinned to her white coat that she was called Dr Lesley Colman and taken in the fact that she was unusually tall as well as slim—a slimness accentuated by the dark trousers she wore under her white coat. She had the unusual combination of hair so fair that in some lights it looked silver, and extremely dark eyes. The more discerning would also have noticed her extreme pallor and the tiny beads of perspiration just above her well-shaped eyebrows as she kept a fixed vigil on a door at the far end of the corridor.

She was so engrossed in her own affairs she was unaware that a man and a woman had come out of a room behind her. With her back to them and her eyes fixed ahead, she didn't even hear them approach. They were one pace behind her and about to overtake when for some reason she was later to regret she took a sudden step backwards. Her leg became entangled with that of the man—she lost her balance and fell flat on her face.

Immediately there came a firm grip on her arm and she was jerked, none too gently, to her feet.

'Sorry, lad, I didn't mean to trip you,' came an admonishing voice, surprisingly deep and rich. 'But you should take more care where you plant your feet. I could have been a patient!'

Lesley spun round, no thought of an apology in her mind—she was too outraged. 'I'm not a lad!' she retorted furiously. 'And you should have looked where you were going!'

The man topped her by about four inches, which made a nice change. She was immediately struck by his appearance, for he was all in navy blue—navy suit, navy rolltop jersey, and by contrast his hair was corn-gold and his eyes a piercing blue. It crossed her mind that he could be a seafarer, he had eyes used to looking into distances and the deep tan of someone used to the outdoors. Now amusement flared into his eyes and his mouth curved into a teasing smile.

'I do apologise for taking you for a feller, I can see my mistake now.' His voice held a hint of mock politeness which made his companion titter.

Lesley treated her to one of her scornful looks, a scorn purely spurious, for at the sight of this girl her stomach had tightened with envy. She was pert and pretty with a button nose and short upper lip that invited kisses. She linked her arm possessively through the man's and appraised Lesley with pale green eyes.

'I'm so sorry, I shouldn't have laughed,' she said soothingly but without a trace of sincerity. She was quite young, about twenty, with reddish-gold hair and long black lashes which she knew how to use effectively. 'And you're *so* tall,' she added, looking up at Lesley's five foot ten. 'And—oh!' she had now noticed the name tab, 'you're a doctor—*Dr* Lesley Colman. You must be clever as well . . .'

'Yes, I'm known as the brain on stilts,' said Lesley frigidly, and this sent the girl off into another fit of giggles. Her companion gave Lesley a look that seemed to see into the inner recesses of her mind, and instantly on her guard, she looked away. No further remarks passed between them, and the couple continued on their way, going through the swing doors that led to the stairs.

Out of sight they were also out of Lesley's mind, leaving only a minor irritation that was soon engulfed by her bigger worry. Surely the appointments committee had come to a decision by now? It was some time since they had started to interview the candidates for the vacancy of senior house surgeon. Dr Barrett had been the last to be seen, she had been one of the first, and she had been so confident when she applied that the job would be hers without question. After all, she had already served her six months as a house surgeon with Sir Walter Reynolds' surgical team and she had hoped that would give her an advantage over the other applicants.

St Bede's in the metropolitan London catchment area was a small teaching hospital with a countrywide reputation, chiefly because of consultants like Sir Walter on the staff. Only the cream of the medical students who studied for their degrees there were ultimately selected to stay on to do their pre-registration year as house officers, and only a very select few of those, once registered, obtained the coveted posts as senior house surgeons or house physicians.

Lesley had taken the prize for the best student of her year and then, when qualified, had made an outstanding house officer, first with a medical team for six months and then the remaining six months of her registration year as a house surgeon with Sir Walter's unit. There was a joke current among the junior staff as to what was foremost about Sir Walter—his paunch or his reputation—and all agreed that his reputation won by inches. Lesley respected him as a great surgeon, though in his presence she always felt ill at ease. A look from his hooded eyes or a curt command could reduce her to a jelly, and he always addressed her as Jane. She had been christened Jane Lesley and it was there on her birth certificate for all to see, but when she was thirteen she had dropped the Jane and refused to answer to any other name but Lesley—a liberty she dared not take with Sir Walter.

When she was thirteen she had heard the charwoman telling her aunt that she was a cross-grained child. 'A right funny mixture, if you ask me—it looks kinda odd, that whitish hair with them dark eyes—a regular plain Jane, if you ask my opinion.'

'But I didn't ask your opinion,' Aunt Celia had answered in her prim fashion; nevertheless she herself remarked to Lesley later that looks weren't important—brains outlasted beauty.

Already selfconscious about her height, Lesley had looked up the word 'cross-grained' in the dictionary and had discovered it meant odd or perverse. Odd—a plain Jane; she could rectify the Jane part even if she couldn't change the colour of her hair or her eyes.

Her aunt's remark about brains outlasting beauty was a nod to the fact that Lesley was always top of her class, but for a girl sensitive about her looks that was poor consolation. She had to put up with some envy from girls not as bright as she was, and when one or two discovered that beneath that outward indifference was a nature vulnerable to spite they were meciless. She was dubbed the 'brain on stilts' at first in fun, but as soon as it was realised how this jarred on her, 'brain on stilts' she became for the rest of her schooldays.

Life was much easier for her at medical school. There she was popular with male and female students alike, and as she was naturally modest about her achievements nobody begrudged her her success. She was regarded as a bit of a loner, and though she had no enemies she had no close friends either, except for James Stimpson, then a surgical registrar, whose wife had been at school with Lesley for a time.

From him the other students learnt all there was to know about her. That she had no relatives except an elderly aunt who was a bit of a recluse and didn't encourage Lesley to bring friends home.

It was to see James that Lesley was now hanging around the first floor corridor at St Bede's, where the Appointments Board were still in conclave in the interview room. James was now a junior consultant, and though not on the Appointments Committee had been asked to sit in. Sir Walter was his chief, and Sir Walter was also Chairman of the Committee.

Lesley knew that just she and one other applicant had been short-listed—a Keith Barrett who had trained at Bart's. Sir Walter was also a Bart's man, but she didn't think that would influence his decision.

She felt she was walking a tightrope, prowling about the corridor waiting for the result. The unfortunate incident with the stranger in navy would have been amusing in different circumstances, but now the slightest interruption to her vigil acted like a rasp on her nerves.

And then the door of the interview room opened and James came out, his short-stepped brisk walk recognisable the length of the corridor. Lesley hurried to meet him and then a few feet away stopped dead in her tracks. His expression told all.

'I didn't get it,' she said flatly.

His chubby face creased into folds of deep regret.

'I'm sorry, Lesley, it went to the Bart's chap.'

She hunched her shoulders. 'Why?'

They fell into step.

'I can't say why. You were both suitable candidates. I thought you had the slight edge, being St Bede's trained—but he had the experience—'

'It's because he's a Bart's man,' said Lesley hotly. 'Or because I'm a woman. Sir Walter is prejudiced against female house officers.'

'Nonsense, Lesley—it wasn't for either of those reasons. Dr Barrett had twelve months' more experience than you; he did an extra six months as a house surgeon and six months in practice. I still think you're the better candidate—but then I'm prejudiced too. I did warn you that applying for this post immediately after registering was being a bit optimistic, but you were so determined—'

'I needed the extra money,' she said bluntly. 'What do I do now? There are no other jobs available in this hospital, and my appointment finishes next week.'

'You know you could locum—especially with the holiday season approaching.' James thought for a bit, then added, 'Have you considered general practice?'

'No, I'm not interested. I want to do hospital work.'

'Wouldn't you be tempted by an idyllic spot on the South Cornish coast? Would that change your mind for you?'

Lesley stopped and confronted him, her eyes accusing. James looked away; he never felt comfortable having to look up to her. He took her arm and they walked on.

'I know that tone of voice,' she said. 'It means you're cooking something up. Just's what's on your mind?'

'Nothing much—it's only that an old pal came to see me today. He runs a busy practice in a spot called Trevaise—that's somewhere near Falmouth. He has a partner and until recently an assistant, but she left to get married. Neil Rodway was a fellow student with me and trained here at St Bede's—that's why he's up here for a couple of days, looking likely applicants over. He wants a St Bede's man—or woman,' he added hastily.

Lesley was listening with half an ear. She wondered why James bothered to go into all this when he knew her ambitions to become a surgeon. She shrugged indifferently.

'I'm not interested, James. It's not what I want.'

'But you want a job.'

She thought of the fees of the Belvedere Nursing Home where Aunt Celia was a patient, now overdue.

'I must get a job,' she said desperately.

'Then just see Dr Rodway, I'm sure he'll make you change your mind. It's only for six months. He's got someone else lined up to start in September, and by then there'll be two senior house surgeons' jobs vacant here and I know you'll get one of them. Keep in mind, Lesley, that six months in practice did Keith Barrett no harm. It got him the job you coveted.'

The point went home. Lesley gave him a long hard look from beneath her lashes.

'That was a crafty one,' she said with a half-smile. 'Anyway, why are you so keen on me getting this Cornish job?'

If he had told her the reason why she would have shied

away from the idea like a startled filly, so he kept it to himself. But he talked it over with his wife that evening. Lesley had been invited to supper—it was ready now and keeping hot in the hostess trolley—four-year-old Amy was in bed and Lesley due any moment.

'You want Lesley to get this job. You think it would do her good—why?' Karen Stimpson asked her husband. She was sitting on an old-fashioned couch on one side of a blazing fire, some crochet-work idle in her hands, while James stretched out in a deep leather chair opposite. There was no other illumination in the room but the firelight, and its softening glow did little to reveal Karen's swollen body. She was seven months pregnant.

They often sat like this of an evening. They both had placid contented natures and enjoyed the comfort of their substantial Victorian home, sharing it at intervals with their closest friends.

At Karen's question James stared thoughtfully into the fire. 'She needs to get away from the hospital for a time,' he said musingly. 'She doesn't spare herself and the work is taking over her life. She doesn't even eat regularly—there isn't a spare inch of flesh on her body.'

'Perhaps she can't afford to eat,' said Karen softly.

James stared. 'Rubbish! You and I got married on what she earns now, and she's living cheap in that hostel.' He stopped, struck by a sudden idea. 'Is that why you invite her over so often? Just to feed her up? Wherever did you get hold of the idea that she's starving herself?'

'I didn't say she's starving herself. I just think she doesn't eat as sensibly as she should. What do you know about her private life, James—apart from that old aunt down in Sussex? Has she any other relatives?'

'She's never mentioned any—but then she's a bit cagey about her own affairs. I sometimes get the impression that she's got some big worry on her mind, but she never talks about it—'

'She wouldn't. Lesley can always make time to listen to others' troubles, but she keeps her own to herself.' Karen got up from the couch with some difficulty. 'Oh, I wish Junior would stop kicking,' she moaned, holding her back. 'I'm sure it's a he and that he's going to be a footballer. Hurry on May—I can't wait!'

'As long as Junior can wait,' said James, grinning. 'Want any help?'

'No, thanks—it's easier to do things myself than stop to explain where everything is to you. But do remember to give Lesley a drink as soon as she arrives, not like last time when you sat her down and talked shop.'

Karen went off to the kitchen, switching on the sitting-room lights as she passed the door, while James did his duty as a host, thrusting a glass of sherry upon Lesley before she had even shed her coat. With his wife's words in mind he watched as Lesley ate her dinner. She ate well and with enjoyment—Karen was a good cook. The beef and mushroom casserole was spiced with a delicate flavour of herbs, and to follow was raspberry tart and cream and then cheese and biscuits.

'There's one more helping of tart left, could you finish it up?' Karen asked Lesley, ignoring the questing signal in her husband's eye.

'I wish I could, it was delicious, but I couldn't manage another mouthful. Your pastry is always so light—what's the secret, Karen?'

'Cool hands and a cool head, I guess,' answered Karen, laughing. 'Now, coffee—'

'No,' said Lesley, rising and pushing back her chair.

'I'm going to wash up first, then we can sit and have our coffee with clear consciences.'

This time Karen did not ignore her husband's signal. 'I think James was hoping to have a word with you first.'

Lesley gave James one of her long cool looks. 'I know what he wants to say to me, he's been on to me about it all afternoon. It can wait—I'm washing up first.'

Though Karen was ordered to sit down with her feet up she followed Lesley out to the kitchen. 'Well then, let me talk to you instead,' she said as she helped herself to a clean tea-towel out of a drawer. 'Why don't you want to discuss this Cornish job with James?'

Lesley washed and rinsed several dishes before answering.

'There's no point,' she said at last. 'I've no intention of going into general practice. You know I've always wanted to be a surgeon.'

'Neil Rodway was—is a fine surgeon himself. He would have made quite a reputation if he'd stayed on here—but Cornwall has a strong pull for him and he never regretted becoming a GP.'

'You seem to know a lot about this Dr Rodway.'

Karen smiled. 'I should do—he was a friend of James and came to our wedding. We don't see much of him now—he rarely comes up from Cornwall. All his interests are down there.'

'What's he like?' asked Lesley.

'You mean to look at? He's a tall, blond Viking of a man about James' age—thirty-six—'

Lesley froze, her arms up to the elbows in soapy water. She had just experienced a rare flash of insight. 'Actually I didn't mean his looks,' she said slowly, 'I meant his character—but I think I can describe him. He's about six feet two, has corn-coloured hair, very straight and thick, and vivid blue eyes. Accompanied by a giggling little scrap of nonsense five foot nothing with red hair and false eyelashes about an inch long.' Her voice was so brittle, Karen stared at her in surprise.

'You've met him?'

'To be more accurate, we collided,' Lesley corrected. 'He picked me up off the ground and brushed me down and addressed me as lad. I could have punched him!'

At that Karen laughed. 'Well, if you will go about in trousers all the time, what do you expect? Yes, that's Neil all right—you've described him to a T. I don't know anything about the bit of nonsense he had with him, but I'm not surprised—females hang around Neil like bees round a honeypot.'

'I'm not surprised either—he looks the type who likes to have his ego bolstered,' said Lesley dryly. She rubbed her hands on the kitchen towel with more vigour than was necessary. 'Shall we make the coffee now? James will be wondering what's happened to it.'

But Karen was not to be put off so easily. Her eyes, which were grey and humorous, had a determined glint to them.

'Lesley, what is this with you where men are concerned? You're either hail-fellow-well-met like you are with James or else you give them the cold shoulder. Aren't you interested in men as men?'

An unamused smile played about Lesley's sensitive mouth. 'What you really mean is why haven't I got a boy-friend—is there anything wrong with me? I suppose from your point of view there is—because I just haven't got time for romance, not yet. I have a career to carve for myself first, and getting a senior house surgeon's post was the first rung on the ladder. I expect James has already told you I didn't get the job I wanted, so now I have to do some rethinking—but not now. It's been a hard day and I'm tired.'

Karen hardened her heart, telling herself it was for Lesley's own good. 'It's a good thing James didn't think like that—we had a real struggle when we first got married, but we made it, and I don't think it hampered his career one bit. You sometimes have to take risks to get what you really want.'

Lesley didn't answer. She stared fixedly at the floor, unable to meet Karen's candid eyes. Karen knew her better than anyone else, and Karen was deceptively perceptive. She touched Lesley on a raw spot by saying, 'You're not still sensitive about being called a plain Jane, are you? How many years ago was that—eleven—twelve? Have you forgotten what happened to the Ugly Duckling?'

Lesley gave a despairing sigh. 'Karen dear, I know you mean well and that you're trying to boost my morale after a pretty rotten day, but really, I'd much rather not talk about it—not tonight.' And as if that was the end of the matter she turned her back on her friend and busied herself with the cups and saucers, filled the coffee-pot, spooned coffee from a canister and took down a sugar bowl from the dresser.

She was as much at home in Karen's kitchen as she was in the bed-sitting room she occupied at the hostel. More so. It was a charming old-fashioned room which the Stimpsons had furnished in keeping with its Victorian image, and it reminded her of the one in her aunt's house in Wimbledon. Such twentieth-century appliances as a washing machine and fridge and freezer were kept out of sight in the utility room, which had once been a scullery. Karen watched her in silence, then decided to make one more attempt to break through her reserve.

'I wish you'd have a real hard look at yourself some time and try to get rid of this image you have of yourself as being some kind of freak! My God, Lesley, you don't know how fortunate you are. You've got legs up to your armpits—you've got those beautiful hollow cheeks that top models crave. Do you know, some of them have their back teeth extracted to get that effect? You've got hair like floss and it would look fantastic if you would only treat it right. For goodness' sake, where do you get it cut?'

'I don't have it cut.'

'You mean somebody actually chews it for you!'

Lesley tried to keep a straight face but failed. 'I mean I cut it myself.'

'And it jolly well looks like it! Whatever do you do with your money!'

The minute she said it Karen was sorry, especially when she saw the colour run up into Lesley's pale cheeks. 'I'm sorry—that was rude. It's no business of mine what you do with your money.' She came closer and put a tentative hand on Lesley's arm. 'Think about this job in Cornwall,' she coaxed. 'Don't hide yourself away in hospitals and hostels. There's a whole wide world out there—and you're only twenty-four. Go out and grasp life with both hands, Lesley—go out and make friends.'

That evening Lesley left earlier than her usual time, making an excuse that she had some letters to write which didn't deceive either Karen or James. There had been an uncomfortable silence to accompany their coffee, and it was something of a relief to Karen to hear the door shut behind her. James walked her to the bus stop. It had just started to rain, and when he came back he was shaking the moisture from his coat before hanging it in the cloakroom.

'I expect you tried to persuade Lesley to take a taxi,' Karen said as soon as he sat down. He leant forward and poked the fire before answering.

'I didn't—it would have been a waste of time. Anyway, the bus will put her down near the hostel and she was wearing that old Burberry, she'll be all right.' He helped himself to some more coffee which was keeping warm in the hearth.

'Did you get the chance to mention Cornwall again?'

'I did—and this time she promised to sleep on it. I'm not very hopeful, but at least it wasn't a flat refusal as before.' James looked across at his wife with a tender smile. 'What did you say to her, witch, to make her change her mind?'

Karen shrugged. 'Too much, I'm afraid—you know me once I get going. Oh, James, I do wish Lesley could meet someone like you and settle down. Marriage is so good with the right partner, I hate to think what she's missing. And she'd be much better off in a cosy home like ours than in that dreary hostel.'

James shook his head. 'I don't know what sort of life there is in store for Lesley, but I do know it won't be cosy,' he said with conviction.

Far from sleeping on the idea of the job in Cornwall, Lesley hardly slept at all. Karen's remarks had sparked off memories of her childhood she was trying to forget.

There had been no love lost between Lesley and her aunt, in fact for many years Lesley had convinced herself that she hated her father's elderly sister. There had been resentment on both sides when on the deaths of her parents she had been taken to the only home available to her—the old house in Wimbledon. Life had then taken on a grim aspect for the ten-year-old child suddenly deprived of love and indulgence and a happy-go-lucky style of living, and she had been far too young and too shocked by grief to understand the disruption a strange child could make in the orderly existence of a spinster aunt.

It was from that time that Lesley had learnt to control her feelings, shutting her emotions behind an impassive look which her aunt mistook for sulkiness. They had more in common than they realised, the severe-looking woman and the silent child. Both were adept at keeping their worries to themselves.

Celia Colman was old enough to be her niece's grandmother. She was more than twenty years older than her half-brother and had known what it was to be an unloved child herself. When her widowed father had married again, this time to a girl not much older than his daughter, she had been sent to care for an elderly relative in the north of England, only meeting her stepmother again at the christening of baby Patrick. Then she had returned to the North until the death of her father's cousin had released her from her duties. By this time her father was widowed again, and needing someone to look after him, sent for Celia. Patrick was now living in a commune in America. When her father died he left her the home and its contents and a small allowance, but the bulk of his money went to his son. This brought Patrick back to England to marry the girl he had known at college, and then the excited pair went off for an extended honeymoon to remote parts of the world.

Celia had sacrificed her young years looking after elderly relatives—now what remained of her life was her own. She didn't ask for much—her wants were modest.

Books, music, her garden, and an occasional holiday. All this Lesley was to learn many years later from old letters and diaries.

Lesley had been a pupil at a boarding school in Hertfordshire when she was suddenly orphaned. Aunt Celia saw no reason why her education should be interrupted, so she stayed on—but with a difference: her pocket-money was halved and her uniforms were only replaced when they had grown indecently short.

This indication of her aunt's tight-fistedness and the humiliation it caused added to Lesley's resentment. When she left school and said she wanted to study medicine she saw a look of horror come into her aunt's eyes which she would remember for the rest of her days.

'I think it would be more suitable for you to train as a secretary,' Aunt Celia said coldly. 'A good secretary is never without work.'

'Neither is a good doctor,' retorted Lesley. 'If you're worried about the cost of my training and the fact that I won't be earning for nearly five years—I vow I'll pay you back every penny when I do start making money.'

Aunt Celia went white.

'There's no question of that—I know my duty. You must do as you think fit.'

So Lesley started her training at St Bede's Medical School, and life at home took on a new dimension. Aunt Celia had never indulged in luxuries—now even necessities were pared down. Holidays and outings became a thing of the past, and then some of the better pieces of furniture began to disappear. Next went some good watercolours and then the silver. When Lesley asked about them Aunt Celia said in an offhand way that she was getting past polishing and caring for such things. The cleaning woman had stopped coming years before.

It wasn't until much later that Lesley was able to connect the disappearance of these articles with the times when she had needed a set of instruments or expensive textbooks, or the fees for an exam. By this time Aunt Celia was past understanding and being cared for in a nursing home.

It was towards the end of her training, just after she had passed her Second MB, that she realised her aunt was behaving oddly and having sudden lapses of memory. But it was only after the police found her on the main highway wandering along in the rain in her slippers and without a coat that Lesley realised that something would have to be done. First she consulted her aunt's doctor, then the solicitor.

Dr Thomas told her there were two courses open to her—to give up her studies and stay at home to devote herself to her aunt, or to put her aunt into care. He advised the latter. He had always taken an interest in Lesley's career and thought it a crime to consider giving it up.

Mr Thurston's advice was more to the point. 'Your aunt needs the kind of attention you're not capable of providing,' he said bluntly. 'She'd be better off in a home.'

Lesley felt stunned. 'Do—do you know of a good nursing home for her?'

'A nursing home is out of the question. The best thing for you to do is get in touch with the Social Services people and they'll take charge of your aunt—find her a place in one of the homes run by the local authorities—'

'But Aunt Celia can afford a *private* nursing home. She must have lots of money, she was always so careful.'

Lesley was never to forget the look Mr Thurston gave her.

'You don't know much about your aunt's personal affairs, do you? For years she's been ekeing out a living for the two of you on a shrinking income. She doesn't even own this house any more—she took out a mortgage on it before your father's death. I advise you to go through her papers, you'll find them most revealing.'

He was right. They told Lesley everything. There were diaries, letters, invoices, bills—Aunt Celia had kept everything, and among them a bundle of letters from her young half-brother covering a span of eighteen years, and each one with the word 'Answered' written on the envelope in Aunt Celia's small, tight writing.

Gradually as Lesley read through them another picture of her father began to emerge—an engaging, light-hearted man with a come-easy go-easy attitude to life and ever on the lookout to make an easy and quick fortune. Nearly all the letters contained a plea for money as well as a fervent account of his latest venture.

It was a long and bitter day for Lesley as she came to terms with the realisation that the money her beloved father had spent so lavishly on her and her mother had all come from Aunt Celia. Even the car that had caused the fatal accident was not their own—it had been obtained, but not paid for, in her aunt's name.

This, then, was the reason for Aunt Celia's supposed meanness—she just hadn't had the money any more. Yet she had gone on selling off her possessions to pay for her niece's education and later her medical training. Not out of love—she had no experience of love—but from a strong sense of family duty.

Lesley was not one to cry, she had hardly shed a tear since the night of her parents' deaths, but now she broke down and wept bitterly. She despised herself for not being able to offer her aunt any love, and could not even now. All she felt was a compassion and the resolve to make up to her somehow for all her years of self-sacrifice.

Her first task was to find a suitable nursing home. After many enquiries she settled on the Belvedere in Sussex. When she was told what the fees were, she quailed, but it was a luxurious place in a beautiful setting and she knew her aunt would have the best of care and attention. In spite of Mr Thurston's pessimism there was some money over after the sale of the Wimbledon house and its contents, enough to keep her aunt for the next two years. Lesley herself had moved into the hostel. It was cheaper than renting private rooms and as it was attached to the hospital she saved on fares.

By the time she was qualified and earning money there was very little left of her aunt's estate, and from now on the nursing home fees swallowed up every penny remaining after paying her own expenses. It was because of this that she had banked on getting the senior house officer's post. In spite of the pretence she had created of not caring two hoots for her appearance she longed for the chance to go into a store and order the clothes her heart hankered after.

Only that morning she had received a letter from the Matron of the Belvedere to say that unavoidably the fees were having to be increased by fifteen pounds a month, but that if Lesley agreed Miss Coleman could be moved to a double room then instead of an increase the amount would be decreased. But Lesley closed her mind to that suggestion; she still had a lot of guilt to atone for.

For this reason alone a job in general practice was a temptation, though she disliked the idea of moving so far from London. She wouldn't be able to continue her visits to her aunt either—not that from her aunt's point of view that mattered. Aunt Celia had long since ceased to recognise her niece. She lived contentedly in a world of her own.

When, on the following morning, James again tackled her about meeting Dr Rodway, this time she agreed, and an appointment was made for twelve-thirty as he planned to return to Cornwall later that afternoon. She still wasn't sure in her own mind whether she would accept the assistantship if it were offered to her. She wanted to see Dr Rodway again, to assess the impression he made on her the second time round. She still carried an image of a man in navy blue whose blue eyes seemed to have the capacity to penetrate her inner thoughts. She found this disturbing. If she didn't feel comfortable in his presence there was no point in working for him, no matter how liberal the reward.

At ten-thirty she headed for the canteen in search of a much-needed cup of coffee. She had just finished a session in Outpatients attending Sir Walter's clinic, and the Chief had been in one of his more caustic moods.

The canteen was nearly empty, but she took her coffee to a table screened by trelliswork supporting a variegated ivy. The Management Committee had decided that greenery placed at strategic points would soften the purely functional appearance of the plastic chairs and tables. It was characteristic of Lesley that she liked to hide away even at mealtimes. The coffee was hot and strong and she took it black at this time of day. She had drunk about half when the door opened and James appeared, and with him Neil Rodway.

They stood looking about them, the tall blond giant dwarfing the tubby junior consultant, then James pointed to a table on the other side of the screen and they walked towards it.

Lesley shrank back behind the foliage; the table was within earshot and she wasn't at all sure she couldn't be seen. She didn't want to meet again like this—she wasn't prepared.

As soon as the two men were seated with their coffee they began to talk, and the subject was herself. It was too late now to reveal her whereabouts. She stared down bleakly into her cup.

'You won't regret it,' said James. 'She's the brains of her year and a dedicated worker. She should have got the senior house post, it was a damn shame she was passed over, but it could mean your gain.'

There was a moment's silence, then came the deep, slightly amused voice Lesley found irksome. 'I can't say I was very impressed with what I saw of her. I prefer a woman to look like a woman.'

Lesley's hands clenched in her lap. Her heart began to pound, stifling her breathing. This was what came of playing the eavesdropper!

'It was just unfortunate you had that encounter,' said James. 'It's a bit unfair to make a snap judgment on that.'

'She was so uptight too—referring to herself as a brain on stilts! I can't say I think a neurotic bluestocking is a suitable GP to let loose on my patients.'

'Come off it, Neil, she's not neurotic. She's one of the most level-headed people I know. As for that unfortunate phrase, brain on stilts—that's just something that rankles from her schooldays. I wouldn't have blamed her for saying something stronger in the circumstances, she was a bit wound up waiting for the verdict of the Appointments Committee. And it shows a sensitive side to her nature too. You wouldn't want someone completely insensitive let loose on your patients, I presume!'

Lesley believed if James made one more excuse for her she would scream. There came another silence, then:

'All right, I'll consider her. The chap I saw yesterday is no good, so I only hope she's all you crack her up to be. There is one thing in her favour—she'll go down well with my women patients. I mean she won't be any threat to their boy-friends or husbands, quite unlike her predecessor. She was a right little sexpot!'

Lesley sat on long after the two men had left. Her coffee cooled in its cup while she stared at it unseeingly. Neil Rodway's cruel words rankled worse than the silly nickname given to her by her schoolmates, and the hurt was worse because she knew it was true. She wasn't physically attractive to men. An image of the man in the navy suit came to her mind—she saw his amused blue eyes, his arrogant smile, and she suddenly slammed her hands together in a passion of rage.

'Damn you—damn you!' she cried, and she didn't care if the counter staff heard. 'I'll take your wretched job—and I'll make you eat your words. So I'm not a sexpot! You wait—Oh, you wait, Dr Neil Bigheaded Rodway!'

CHAPTER TWO

By the time Lesley went back on duty she was her outwardly calm-looking self again. She was professional enough to be able to put all but immediate problems out of her mind, and she now had to see three patients on the men's surgical ward who were due for operations that afternoon.

Two of the three were minor straightforward cases, one a ganglion in the foot and the other a Dupuytren's contracture—the contraction of a tendon in the hand following a severe burn. But old Mr Matthews in Ward Six was in a different category. He had a history of heart trouble and was having an operation for an inguinal hernia. A quietly-spoken man with an uncomplaining attitude to life, he greeted Lesley with a wan smile.

'This is the big day at last, Doctor,' he said with an attempt at levity. 'One good thing about it, I shan't know what's going on. When I wake up it will be all over.'

Lesley drew the curtain around his bed and sat down beside him.

'That's just what I've come to talk about, Mr Matthews. Because of your heart condition it's been decided to give you a spinal anaesthetic instead of a general.'

A flicker of alarm crossed his face.

'What will that mean?'

'It means instead of you going unconscious you'll be aware of what's going on all the time throughout the operation. But you won't feel anything—just drowsiness.'

'No pain at all?' Mr Matthews seemed incredulous.

'Just a small prick in your back when the anaesthetic is administered—and after that you'll be numb from the waist down and won't feel a thing, I can promise you. And you won't have any of the after-effects of a general anaesthetic. No dry mouth or excessive thirst, no nausea—just a feeling of numbness in the legs which may last ten to twelve hours—but apart from that you'll be fine.'

He looked reassured.

'Thank you, Doctor. I know you're not just saying that to please me. You don't look the sort to fool an old man. No pain, eh?'

'Some discomfort from the wound, as you might expect, but Sister will give you something for that.' Lesley got up from the chair and opened the curtains again. 'I'll have a bet with you, Mr Matthews. You'll be sitting up in bed enjoying your supper tonight—'

She was interrupted by a bleeping noise from her pocket. Mr Matthews grinned.

'Never a dull moment, eh, Doctor?'

'You're right.' She patted him on the shoulder and hurried away to the nearest phone, wishing all her patients were as amenable. When she got through to the switchboard she was told Mr Stimpson wanted to speak to her. She asked to be put through to him.

'Hallo there, Lesley.' James sounded in a hearty mood. 'Just making sure you haven't forgotten your appointment.'

Lesley couldn't hide her annoyance. She could not forget the part James had played in the conversation she had overheard.

'I haven't forgotten, and there's still ten minutes to go

until half-past twelve. What's the rush?'

'You sound curt. Anything bothering you, Les?'

'Only you. I was with a patient when you had me buzzed.'

'Sorry—sorry! I just wanted to let you know that Neil Rodway will see you here in my office—'

'Thank you. I'll be along in time.' She spoke with more composure than she was feeling.

Ten minutes gave her time to freshen her face and tidy her hair. The only other occupant of the cloakroom was one of the nurses, a pretty, dark little girl applying fresh lip-gloss. An impulse came over Lesley to ask to borrow some, an impulse she at once quashed, imagining the girl's amazement and, possibly, amusement too. She bit her lips instead, and when the nurse had gone she pinched her cheeks, something she had seen her aunt do many times. But her hair! There was nothing she could do about her hair. She could see what Karen meant—it did look chewed.

At twelve-thirty precisely she tapped on the door of James' office and went in. Neil Rodway was there alone, sitting at James' desk reading some papers. He looked up and asked her to take the seat opposite.

She felt slightly disconcerted. She had expected James to be present, though common sense told her that having made the introductions James could play no further part in the proceedings. Still, she would have welcomed his support. She had not wanted to be alone with this man whose scathing words were still ringing in her mind—'I prefer a woman to look like a woman!'

His very manner of dress intimidated her. He was still all in navy—was it because it highlighted the gold of his hair? If so that meant he was vain. And those brilliant eyes—so blue, so far-reaching in their intensity—did he really have to stare at her like that? There was a ghost of a smile playing about his mouth, and she had to concede that he was very good-looking. Not that men like him interested her—she felt more at home with the shy, academic type.

Dr Rodway put his elbows on the table and leaned forward. 'I've just been reading all about you—very impressive. I understand you have a busy schedule today. It's good of you to give up some of your precious time for this interview.'

She thought he was being sarcastic. 'Three operations from the same ward might seem busy to someone from a country practice,' she said crisply.

He let that pass. 'I'll be brief, then. There are just some preliminary questions I'd like to shoot at you first. I know all I need to know about your proficiency as a doctor, but there are just one or two extra details I'd like to get clear.'

He began to 'shoot' his questions, starting at first with innocuous enquiries about her hobbies, if any—what did she do in her spare time, what kind of holidays did she like best. It only gradually dawned on her that he was probing into her private life, but when he got on to the subject of her parents and their early deaths she quickly snapped out of her hynoptic-like trance, angry more with herself than with him for the mesmerising effect his deep rich voice was having on her.

She interrupted him. 'I can't see what all this is leading up to. What bearing it can possibly have on a job not lasting more than six months? If all you want is a character reference you have only to apply to the Dean.'

He lolled back in his chair, one hand drumming on the desktop. He didn't take his eyes from hers.

'I know you're a good doctor and were an excellent

student—that's all here,' he flicked at the notes, 'but I'm looking for something else—not a character reference. What I mean is, I want to know what makes you tick.'

Lesley didn't need artificial aids to redden her cheeks then. 'And just what do you mean by that?' she demanded.

'I mean will you fit in with the rest of us down at Trevaise? We're something of a closed shop in our little community. We meet our patients socially as well as professionally. Here, in a fairly large hospital, you don't have your patients long enough to experience a meaningful relationship with them. In practice we see the same ones year after year.' He quickly forestalled her as she made an attempt to interrupt. 'I know it will be for six months only, but a disruptive six months could cause lasting damage. What I'm trying to say is—will you fit in?'

She felt her mouth set in an obstinate manner. It was a look her Aunt Celia would have recognised from her early years. 'I'll do my duty as a doctor. I'll tend my patients faithfully. I'll work all hours. I can't promise more than that,' she said coldly.

Dr Rodway's expression hardened.

'I'm sorry about that,' Dr Colman,' he said crisply. 'In all other respects your credentials are faultless, we could have done with a doctor like you on our staff. But there, it's not to be. All the same, thank you for sparing me some of your time.' He stood up.

Lesley also rose, feeling a sense of outrage sweep over her. She had convinced herself he would fall over himself to obtain her services—now it sounded as if she was being dismissed.

'You're not offering me the appointment?' she asked.

'Regretfully, no.'

'May I ask why?' Her voice matched his, her eyes were black with anger.

'I didn't think I would have to spell it out. I just can't afford to have a disruptive element in the practice, and I don't think you'll be suitable.'

She swallowed back the words of fury that rushed to her lips. She wouldn't demean herself to argue with this ice-block of a man. Then unbidden came the thought of Aunt Celia and the bill from the Belvedere awaiting payment. In spite of her protests to the contrary, she had been hoping to land this job. For a time she had believed it was hers just for the asking—for a time she had planned to make this arrogant man reverse his opinion of her. Those plans vanished now, overtaken by panic as it came to her with renewed force that soon she would be another statistic in the ranks of the unemployed, and it wasn't unusual these days for young doctors to be without work.

Her mouth turned suddenly dry. It was vital that she did get this vacancy—there was nothing else for her in the hospital pipeline, and though James was sure she would be next in line for a senior house job, that was six months away. In the meantime, she had to live, and Aunt Celia had to be cared for.

She swallowed hard and sat down again. Surprised, Dr Rodway also seated himself. 'Yes?' He had a habit of raising one eyebrow when he queried anything.

Very effective and affected, thought Lesley disdainfully, but she kept such thoughts well hidden when she addressed him. If she had to play on this man's ego to get the job, then play on it she would.

'I'm very sorry I gave you the impression that I'm a disruptive influence,' she said. 'I'm—I'm not at my best at interviews. My—my nerves play me up.' The very word nerve grated on her ears. Nerves indeed!—she liked to think she didn't know the meaning of the word.

Dr Rodway gave her a look that seemed to dissect her mind, and she knew she hadn't fooled him for a moment. He flicked through her notes again. 'You've always interviewed well in the past. What's so different about this time?'

You are! she wanted to shout at him, but she looked modestly down at her hands,

'I need this job,' she said, and there was no mistaking the sincerity in her voice.

'You want to get away from London?'

'No, it's not that. It's the money.'

He gave a slight smile. 'We haven't come to that side of things yet, but yes—the money would be better than you get here, or would even expect as a senior house officer.' He hesitated. 'Are you saving for anything special—like marriage?' His eyes weren't completely guileless.

Lesley felt herself shrinking back into her shell. 'I have commitments. I owe money,' she said bluntly.

He was silent for a while thinking, then he raised his head again, looking straight at her.

'I'll be honest with you, Dr Colman. I'm not happy about taking you on, even though I have a high opinion of you as a doctor. But the job is yours, if you want it—providing you try to do something about that chip on your shoulder before you join us. I wasn't being offensive,' he added hastily, seeing the colour flare into her face again. 'Perhaps I used the wrong phrase. I should have said, please try to get rid of your hang-ups. I mean, from a purely professional point of view, with fifty per cent of my patients the root of all their troubles is psychological. Would a doctor who is herself beset with psychological problems be the right person to deal with them?'

'She could be that much more understanding because of it,' said Lesley with feeling.

He gave her a keen look at that, then his expression lightened. 'You may well be right—anyway, we can give it a try. Now shall we get down to the important part—your salary and other arrangements?' He was back to his half joking, half sardonic way of speaking.

Lesley had only left the room a few minutes when James walked in.

'I saw Lesley in the corridor. She didn't stop, but I didn't think she was looking very pleased. Did she get the job?'

'Yes—but I can't help thinking, James, that she doesn't want to come and work for me any more than I want her. But she needs the money and I need a good assistant. Not a promising start to a relationship, would you think?'

James grinned. 'You could always exercise your charm and win her over.'

Neil grimaced. 'Not a hope.' Then a contemplative look came over his face and his eyes glittered. 'But what a challenge!'

For Lesley the next two weeks went by with alarming quickness. Her own affairs were speedily put in order, she gave in her notice at the hostel—not the customary four weeks, that was waived in the circumstances, as there was always a waiting list for vacancies. Her aunt's affairs took longer. During her last week she went down to Sussex to say goodbye to her.

It was a fine day in early spring. As the bus took her across the South Downs Lesley watched fleecy clouds blowing lazily across a pale blue sky. During the walk to the Belvedere a lark took flight, mounting the sky with fluttering wings and trilling as it soared. Life was bursting out afresh in the hedgerows, and she realised how much more healthy it was for her aunt here than in the old dark house in London that over the years had become more and more hemmed in by busy roads.

She found Aunt Celia in one of her rare lucid moments. She was sitting in an easy chair by the window staring out over the valley, looking her usual picture of neatness. Her white hair gleamed in the faint sunshine, her faded eyes were calm and unafraid. She was wearing the wine-coloured silk dress Lesley had bought her for Christmas with a lightweight woollen shawl across her shoulders. She was well looked after.

Lesley filled a vase with the daffodils she had brought, then went over to sit opposite her aunt, waiting for the inevitable stare of non-recognition. But this time it didn't happen. Her aunt smiled. Unexpectedly she said, 'You look tired, Jane dear. You've been working too hard. You should come and stay with me here—the rest would do you good.'

It was the first time her aunt had used an endearment or shown concern for her, and tears of surprise and pleasure stung her eyes. 'Aunt Celia—you know me! You've recognised me!'

But the moment had passed. The curtain of oblivion rolled back into place and Aunt Celia relapsed into her former role of friendly stranger. But that moment had been enough to make Lesley realise many things. Aunt Celia meant more to her than she had ever thought possible. That love was stronger than guilt—even stronger than duty. This frail woman was all the family she possessed—and they had much in common. They could both love, given the chance; they had both made sacrifices because of the strong ties of family; they had both known loneliness—and all this had drawn them closer together. She sat for a long time after that, holding on to the thin veiny hands, not knowing at the time that it was the last afternoon of peace she was to know for some weeks.

After that visit came a shopping trip to London with Karen. Of course, there had been the usual argument between them first, Lesley insisting she had no money to spare for new clothes.

'But you always have money to spare for others,' Karen pointed out. 'Your aunt, for instance, and what about the presents you buy for Amy, *and* that expensive teddy you gave me for Junior? Why can't you be as generous to yourself?'

Lesley's face went blank, as it always did when they got on to personalities, but Karen would not be put off.

'Please let me lend you some money. Don't frown—I said *lend*, not give! I won a Premium Bond prize a short while back and I haven't touched it. I want you to have it and I'm coming along with you to see how you spend it. You can pay me back in instalments or in a lump sum—I don't care which.'

The temptation was too much for Lesley. She had been worried about clothes to take to Trevaise. Her one good suit was getting shabby—not that she wanted to make a good impression on Neil Rodway, it was too late for that, but she didn't want him to think her frumpish either. She was still concerned about Karen's fitness to go shopping, however.

'All those crowded pavements and stores—it won't be good for you. It could bring on a premature labour—'

'Rubbish! I'm more likely to go into labour standing

here arguing with you. And just think of the pleasure it will give me. My grandmother used to say "It's more blessed to give than to receive", and she was a wise old lady.'

'She was also familiar with her Bible,' retorted Lesley dryly. But she was touched by Karen's generosity, and the worry about the nursing home bill receded from her mind. Still, knowing Karen, she should have been prepared for something other than a straightforward shopping spree.

As soon as they came out of the station she was hurried into a taxi and taken off to an address just off Bond Street.

'Why all this mystery—why a taxi?' asked Lesley, staring out at unfamiliar streets.

'Because I know you—you'd have done a bunk if I'd given you a hint. Sit back and relax, this treat is on me.'

Wild notions flashed across Lesley's mind. An expensive restaurant, a hairdressing salon, sauna baths—each idea brought a further sinking of her heart. When the taxi stopped outside a narrow terraced building with window-boxes and she realised it could turn out to be anything from a jewellers to a small private hotel, her spirits dropped to rock bottom.

Karen walked her through a carpeted and scented foyer where they were greeted by a smart young woman in a pale blue uniform.

'Good morning, Mrs Stimpson.' She spoke to Karen as to an old friend. 'How well you're looking. Have you come for another morale booster?'

'Not for myself this time, Hilary—that will have to wait until I get rid of this bow window,' and Karen patted her abdomen. 'This time it's for a friend.' She whispered the rest of the sentence so that Lesley could not hear. Hilary smiled, her eyes swivelled in Lesley's direction with a professional blandness. Lesley gave her one of her looks.

She was then led down carpeted stairs to the basement with Karen holding her arm, supposedly for support, but Lesley suspected to prevent her escaping. They entered a brilliantly lit room as warm and scented and flower-filled as a conservatory. In the centre was an eye-catching table with six seats along each length, each seat with a mirror before it and an assortment of jars and bottles and tubes. Eleven women were already seated before the mirrors as in a hairdressing salon, all wearing crêpe bandeaux to hold back their hair. Lesley was ushered to the vacant chair.

'What is all this?' she whispered fiercely to Karen.

'It's a beauty salon with a difference,' Karen whispered back. 'Here, you apply your own make-up under supervision—then if you like the result you can buy the products upstairs.' She disentangled Lesley's clutching hand and stood back as a girl with her name—Anne—embroidered on her uniform came forward. As Karen began to leave Lesley looked round at her with an anguished expression.

'Don't you dare leave me! You got me into this—you jolly well stay and see it out!'

'But Lesley, I'm tired. I must sit down. I'm going up to the restaurant for a cup of coffee.'

Lesley glared. Karen had no scruples about using her condition when it suited her purpose—she gave a little wave and was gone. Anne came and stood behind her chair and smiled encouragingly at her reflection.

'I was just about to show my ladies how to apply cleansing lotion,' she said.

'I'm not dirty. I gave my face a good scrub this morning!'

Anne ignored that, just as Lesley herself ignored similar remarks from obstreperous patients. She picked up a colourless bottle and a wad of cotton wool. 'You'll find this lotion only mildly astringent—it soothes and cleanses at the same time. Very suitable for delicate skins such as your own.'

Lesley's sense of humour came to her rescue. She gave a thought to the polluted atmosphere she worked and lived in every day. If her skin looked delicate after years of that then all she could say was that it must be as tough as old leather! She applied the lotion vigorously.

'Gently—gently,' Anne admonished. 'And do take care of the tender skin around the eyes. Stroke like this—from the nose outwards.'

The others watched and followed her instructions. Lesley realised there was nobody else there under fifty, which helped to fuel her indignation against Karen anew—yet she found the lotion soothing and it had a pleasant lemony scent which was refreshing. But after that she got hopelessly left behind. She couldn't remember what to administer next—moisturising cream or foundation lotion—and wondered if it really mattered. She had to admit, however, that her appearance was gradually improving. She baulked at the blusher at first, especially when some of the women applied a little to their chins—why not the tip of their noses? she thought impishly—but under Anne's gentle persuasion she gave in and saw for herself what a difference a little artificial colouring made to her pallor. Not even Anne could persuade her to attempt the eye-shadow, though—the range of colours on the chart baffled her. Her neighbour opposite spoke with a strong American accent. Once she looked round the side of her mirror and said to Lesley direct:

'Don't use the eyebrow pencil, honey, it gives too hard a line. Try a little mascara instead—just so, on the tip of the brush—touch up every hair separately if you can. It looks more natural.'

Lesley thought of the times she had been roused from her sleep to see to an urgent case, with not even time for a wash before dressing. To stop and apply mascara hair by hair—she wanted to laugh!

At last they were finished with her. She was given a list of the cosmetics she had used and an information sheet on their correct use in future. If she bought every one suggested she wouldn't have much change out of a week's salary. All the same, as she went off in search of Karen, she thought she might treat herself to the moisturising cream and lipstick and blusher, just to go on with.

Karen gave a squeal of approval when she saw her.

'My God, the difference a little make-up can do—you look ravishing! Come along, now we'll get you something fit enough to wear with your new face.'

It wasn't far to walk to Regent Street, and Karen insisted she *could* walk, though this time it was Lesley who suggested a taxi. They had another altercation in the store, when Karen picked out a lightweight suit in a black and white check with a pencil-slim skirt, and Lesley wouldn't even try it on.

'It would make me look more like a beanpole than I do already,' she complained.

Karen gave an exaggerated sigh. 'You and your phobia about your height! Heavens above, don't you know Ingrid Bergman was five feet nine inches, and it didn't do her any harm. On the contrary.'

'I'm not exactly in the Ingrid Bergman class.'

The assistant thought it time she intervened.

'Would you like to try our new line in co-ordinates, madam? We have some very attractive blouson jackets and you can select the style of skirt you prefer. We have several to choose from.'

Once Lesley had made up her mind she didn't take long over her purchases. She bought two skirts to go with the jacket, one flared and one pleated, also at Karen's urging a midnight-blue velvet waistcoat suit for evening wear. That, as far as she was concerned, completed her wardrobe, but Karen had other ideas. There were jerseys to go with the skirts and blouses to go with the velvet outfit—but they could wait for now. Lunch came first.

The next time the two girls took a trip out together was the day of Lesley's departure for Cornwall. Karen accompanied her to the coach station. A train journey would have been quicker, but the coach took her to within three miles of Trevaise, to a place called Roshaven. Dr Rodway had written giving instructions for the journey and to advise her that he would be waiting for her at the coach stop.

At five o'clock in the afternoon the coach arrived at Roshaven. Lesley got out and looked about her for the tall figure of Dr Rodway.

There was no sign of him. She couldn't believe it. A man of his height stood out easily, and in any case, only a handful of people had come to meet the coach. Now they drifted away, accompanied by the passengers they had been waiting for. The only one remaining was a girl of twelve or thirteen in anorak and track-suit with light brown hair hanging in a single braid down her back. She was chubby, freckled and blue-eyed, and patently anxious.

Lesley felt a surge of frustration. What a welcome after a long and tiring journey—the man hadn't even the politeness to meet her off the coach! She looked about her with hostile eyes. Suddenly the granite cottages and rising hills on the skyline lost their charm, and she wished she had never left London with its noise and bustle and familiar red buses.

There was a bus of sorts waiting on the other side of the square, half the size of a normal single-decker, its handful of passengers staring patiently out of the window, the driver looking bored. Time didn't seem to matter. The engine was running, but the bus waited.

'Excuse me—' the young girl approached her with a diffident manner, 'I'm waiting for someone who should have been on the coach. I hope she didn't get off somewhere else by mistake. Did anyone get off at St Austell or Truro?'

'Several people. You said a she. What does she look like? Perhaps I can remember.'

'Oh, I've never met her, but I do have her description. She's about your age, I think, and she's a doctor—not that that would show outwardly. Except I expect she looks brainy. My brother said—'

Coldly Lesley interrupted, 'Would your brother be Dr Rodway?'

The girl's eyes widened.

'Oh, you don't mean—?'

'I'm afraid I do. I'm Dr Colman,' said Lesley dryly.

'You're not a bit what I expected!'

Lesley ignored the implied compliment. She was shaking with silent fury. Not even to bother to meet her—to send instead this—this *inadequate* schoolgirl!

'I can well imagine what your brother told you to expect,' she said, 'but don't worry, I won't embarrass you by asking you to tell me. All the same, I'm surprised Dr Rodway didn't come.'

The driver of the bus sounded his horn and the girl made a grab at Lesley's sleeve. 'Could you hurry, please, that's our bus. Dave said he'd give me five minutes and no more. We were late in and I thought we'd miss the coach. I bet you're starving, aren't you? I am!'

Starving wasn't exactly the emotion Lesley was feeling. Tired, angry—and yes, longing for a cup of tea. She followed the Rodway girl on to the bus and by the time they had settled themselves and her case at the back they were heading out of the square. Everybody smiled at her and said, 'Good afternoon, Doctor.' She looked at the girl, who beamed back.

'I told them all about you,' she explained with satisfaction.

Lesley sighed. 'Perhaps you could be equally forthcoming and tell me your name.'

'It's Janice, but I prefer to be called Jan. Neil only calls me Janice when he's mad.'

'Well, Jan, would you mind telling me why your brother sent you instead of coming for me himself?'

'Oh, help, didn't I say? He said that was the first thing I must tell you. Oh dear—another fine!' Her face dropped, but not for long. 'Just as he was coming to meet you he got a difficult birth over the phone—the birth wasn't on the phone, but you know what I mean. He had to scoot off, and Chris and Fran have gone to a wedding, to Fran's brother's up at St Ives—Chris is best man and Fran matron of honour, so they couldn't opt out of it—not that they wanted to. But it would have been more convenient to have had it on a Saturday like everybody else does, then I could have gone. But Neil wouldn't let me miss school to go today. He said I'm too far behind as it is.'

Lesley found herself warming to this talkative young girl beside her. She was an extremely likeable child—quite different in character from her brother!

'But you must have had this afternoon off,' she suggested.

'It's half-holiday unless you play games, and I'm not very good at games,' Jan explained.

'Should I know who Chris and Fran are?'

'Oh, didn't I say! That's Dr Chris Watling and he's partner to Neil and Fran is his wife—Chris's wife, I mean, not Neil's. They've been married for ten years, but there are no little Watlings yet. Fran is getting rather fed up about it, but she's frightened to take that fertility pill in case she has six. She said she could cope with three, but six would be ridiculous. She said it was bad enough when Cindy had nine. Cindy's her red setter, or was rather, she got run over last summer. So now Fran needs a baby more than ever.'

Trying to hide her amusement, Lesley settled down to enjoy the remainder of the journey, enlivened as she knew it would be by Jan's wagging tongue. By the time the bus turned into the deep lane that ran steeply into Trevaise she was well acquainted with the Rodway family. Neil was Jan's half-brother, which accounted for the difference in their ages. Her mother was Geoffrey Rodway's second wife, and for business reasons they were now living in Hong Kong. Jan had stayed behind in England to finish her schooling, under the supervision of her brother.

This was a sore point with Jan. 'He's worse than parents,' she confided. 'He's even worse than my headmistress, and that's saying something. The trouble is, he will treat me like a child—he forgets I'm nearly in my teens. I wish he'd punish me like a child, though,' she added gloomily. 'He says I'm too big to spank or to send to bed early, so he fines me instead. Would you believe, I'm in debt to him for the next three months!'

All this Lesley found very illuminating. Just for a short time she felt a sneaking sympathy for Neil Rodway. It couldn't be easy for him being responsible for someone like Jan—neither child nor woman. But she didn't take Jan's complaints against her brother very seriously. That she was extremely fond of her brother was obvious from the warmth in her voice whenever she mentioned him, which was every other minute.

Suddenly the trees opened up and Lesley found herself looking out on to a stretch of blue water. She saw a flotilla of small boats bobbing on their moorings, a small harbour with a huddle of whitewashed cottages close by, of white surf breaking on distant beaches, of rearing cliffs, and rising up beyond the town the hills that sheltered Trevaise from the north.

'We're home,' said Jan.

CHAPTER THREE

It was an hour before sunset when the bus pulled in on the harbour road. The sea was calm. The sun, a low orange ball with fuzzy outlines, glowed dimly through a faint curtain of cloud. The wind that had skirled the dust from the pavements and tossed up the rubbish in the streets of London was here a mere breeze that brought with it the salty tang of the sea. The air felt like silk against Lesley's cheek, and she breathed in deeply, feeling a sense of quiet elation. In the meanwhile Jan was driving a bargain with the lugubrious Dave.

She rejoined Lesley. 'We don't have to worry about your case. Dave said he'll bring it up to the house.'

'That's marvellous. Do I pay him now?'

'It won't cost you anything—except a tip if you like—it's all part of the service.'

Lesley smiled, then followed Jan up a flight of steep steps between two cottages. Narrow lanes and cobbled alleys made a tortuous right of way between a variety of buildings. They passed two inns old enough to be smugglers' hideouts of another age and then, surprisingly, a modern chemist's and hairdressing salon next door to each other.

Jan explained that there was another route to Carn House. The road that encircled the harbour went up through a housing estate at the top of the hill and eventually joined the main highway to the west. She added, 'It would be miles to walk, though. This way is much quicker.'

'But as you said, not easier,' panted Lesley. She paused, resting against the handrail of yet another flight of steps, realising that this proved how out of condition she was. She looked back over the way they had come, over the rooftops to the sea beyond. The sun was on the horizon now, leaving a shimmering gold path in its wake.

The houses they were passing from now on were much larger than the cottages lower down the hill, substantial, more modern and set in expansive gardens. Here, facing south and sheltered from the prevailing winds, was a botanist's paradise where geraniums grew all the year round and great clumps of camellias were just at the end of their bloom. Aubrietia was already in flower, and some tulips and wallflowers in bud. Everything here was nearly a month earlier than in London.

When Carn House came in sight, a massive gloomy-looking house with granite walls and slate roof, Lesley spared a thought for the unfortunate patients who didn't own cars and had to do this climb. They had to be fit to see the doctor! Then Jan told her that the surgery was down by the harbour.

The path up to the front door was between two high banks of rhododendrons, more steps, then a solid-looking front door. It wasn't locked. Jan pushed it open with her shoulder, holding it for Lesley to precede her.

Once inside the gloom was dispelled. The rooms were high-ceilinged and airy. There was modern furniture and signs of comfort and even a modest luxury. The only room in keeping with the exterior was the kitchen, which was the size of a barn with a window small enough for a closet. The house was about eighty years old, built when servants weren't expected to enjoy light or a good view.

There was a large deal table in the centre which must have come with the house, Lesley thought, its top scrubbed to a startling whiteness. Over this Jan spread a damask cloth.

'What would you like first?' she asked. 'To see your room or a cup of tea?'

This was the first time Lesley became aware that she was expected to live *en famille*, and the prospect didn't thrill her. It was bad enough to have to work with Neil Rodway, but to share his home as well! She removed her hat and hung it on a hook on the door, then ran her fingers through her hair. Her head was aching and she was dying for a cup of tea.

'Tea first, please, but let me get it.'

'Certainly not, you're a guest—for tonight anyway. Sit over there by the Aga, I won't take long.'

Lesley had just seated herself and was watching Jan as she reached up for a teapot from one of the dresser shelves, then took some tea-bags out of a canister, when the sound of a car coming to an abrupt stop outside the house arrested both of them. The front door crashed open and a furious voice was heard to bellow:

'Janice, you thieving little delinquent, wait till I get my hands on you! You know what my instructions were. You know what you should have done—'

Jan dropped teapot and tea-bags in one go. Her freckles stood out like pinpoints on her pale face. 'You can make the tea if you like,' she said. 'I—I won't be a minute.'

She was out of the kitchen like a streak. Lesley ran to the window and watched her flying form haring down the garden path, the braid of hair lashing backwards and forwards like a demented snake. She disappeared into a shrubbery, and at the same time the kitchen door swung open and Neil Rodway came striding in, his face taut with fury. He passed Lesley with a cursory glance.

'Good afternoon,' he said, not slowing in his haste to reach the back door. But once there he stopped abruptly as if smitten by a sudden knowledge. He turned and looked at her again.

'My God, it's you! I didn't recognise you—you look different—'

'You mean I don't look like a feller,' Lesley retorted maddeningly.

He came striding back.

'Look here, I haven't got time to play word games with you right now,' he said crisply. 'Do you know where that young criminal has got to? Don't cover up for her,' he added, seeing the denial coming into her eyes. 'I overtook Dave on the road with your case on a trolley. He told me he'd brought you from Roshaven in his bus. Do you know I gave Miss Light-Fingers a fiver to fetch you in a taxi? It was bad enough that I was prevented from meeting you myself—a taxi was the least I could do—and she brought you home in Dave's bus! I'll skin her alive when I lay hands on her!'

'Oh no, you won't. You'll do what you usually do —you'll dock her pocket-money instead. What a miserly thing to do!'

Neil's eyes blazed with fury. He came one step nearer. 'You take me for some kind of skinflint?'

Lesley took a step backwards. 'No, I didn't mean that. But I do think it's wrong to deprive a girl of that age of spending money. It's taking away her only little bit of independence.'

'In other words, you're condoning what she did? What I consider stealing?'

'Certainly not. What I meant was—' Lesley's voice trailed off. How could she explain to this infuriated man the memories she had of her own schooldays and the humiliation and embarrassment she had suffered because of the shortage of pocket-money. Perhaps something of her feelings could be read in her expression, because Neil, after regarding her frowningly for a moment or two, allowed himself a tight-lipped smile.

When he spoke again his tone was more friendly. 'All right, I'll leave Miss Janice for now. I'll have it out with her in the morning. I gather from what you've just said that you know something of our family history. Did she tell you she'll be going to Hong Kong for her summer vacation?'

'She didn't get round to that, though she did mention that your—her parents are living there.'

'Did she also mention that she'll be spending Easter with friends? It can't come soon enough for me. More importantly, did she offer you anything to eat?'

'She was just about to make me a cup of tea.' Both looked across at the teapot lying on its side on the dresser—the tea-bags scattered on the floor. Neil gave a low growl of exasperation.

'Chaos, chaos, nothing but organised chaos!' he muttered between gritted teeth. 'I hope you don't think I run my surgery the same way I run my household. *That* is a model of efficiency.'

'I see nothing chaotic about this kitchen.' Lesley had been wondering who was responsible for its excessive tidiness.

'This is Mrs Hatchet's domain. Unfortunately, like my partner she also had a prior date fixed for today—a family reunion—otherwise there would have been a meal waiting for you. I hope Janice explained why I wasn't able to meet you in Roshaven.'

'She said a difficult birth on the phone.'

Neil laughed in spite of himself. 'Yes, a first birth and

a breech presentation. The mother is only eighteen and has a very narrow pelvis—there was nothing I could do for her but get her straight into hospital. It may come to a Caesarean—I promised to call back and see how she's getting on.' He gave a hasty glance at his wrist-watch. 'Look, I must make up to you for this lack of hospitality. There's a good seafood restaurant in the town. What about it?'

But the last thing Lesley wanted at the moment was to dine out. She was tired, felt dishevelled, and in need of a wash or, better still, a bath. 'Just a cup of tea, really.' She wondered how many more times she would have to say that before it materialised.

He looked round the kitchen in a hopeless sort of way. 'There's a ham somewhere—Mrs Hatchet was cooking it yesterday. Would that do?'

'If she wouldn't mind me cutting into it, it would do marvellously. Mrs Hatchet is—?'

'My housekeeper. Would you make the tea while I'm carving?'

There was no ham in the fridge. 'I don't know where she's put it,' said Neil Rodway gloomily. He sat down heavily on one of the chairs at the table. 'This just isn't my day!'

But Lesley had seen some eggs. 'Would you mind if I made myself an omelette?' she said. 'I'd enjoy that.'

'Would you make me one too, I haven't had any lunch.'

It was intimidating having Neil watching her all the time she was preparing the eggs. Fortunately for her peace of mind he had discarded his all-navy attire and was wearing sand-coloured cords and a fisherman's knit sweater—very informal wear for a doctor, but it suited him. His corn-gold hair was windswept and the laughter lines around his eyes were white against his tan. Lesley took the bowl of eggs across to the dresser and stood with her back to him while she beat them up, added some grated cheese and a pinch of herbs—and then found she couldn't locate an omelette pan. Eventually she discovered where the frying-pan was kept.

She dished the omelette straight from the pan to the table. It had risen beautifully, and she put a generous helping before Neil. He took a mouthful and then another.

'Good lord! You *can* cook!' His amazement was not exactly flattering, she felt.

'Any reason why I shouldn't?' Her tone was sharp.

'Medical expertise, a budding surgeon—is there anything you can't do?'

'Look like a woman?'

Neil glared at her across the table. 'You're not going to let me forget that, are you?' He finished his meal in silence. Lesley was quiet too. The warmth of the kitchen, the effects of the journey, the nervous tension that had gripped her for the past two weeks were now taking their toll. She had difficulty stifling her yawns, and Neil was not slow to notice. He pushed his chair back and got up.

'You need an early night. Come along, I'll show you to your room and then fetch your case. It's in the car.'

'I must clear these things away first—'

'Leave them. Mrs Hatchet can deal with them when she gets in.'

She followed him out of the kitchen, through the wide hall and up the curving staircase. It was a rambling house with floors on different levels. From the upper hall they went up three shallow stairs to a room that jutted out over the front entrance. This had a wide bay window which gave panoramic views of the old town and the harbour. There was a double bed with duvet and flounces in the same material as the curtains, and a wardrobe and dressing-table in a pale creamy wood. Also a set of bookshelves and a desk—and best of all to Lesley at that moment, an en-suite bathroom. The fitted carpet was a dusty pink that picked out the main colour of the bedcover and curtains. She felt overwhelmed by the splendour.

'I think you'll be comfortable here,' said Neil. He had fetched her case from the car and now dropped it on the desk, oblivious of its polished surface. 'My stepmother and father sleep here where they're home—they like the view.' He walked to the door. 'I'm off to the hospital now. If there's anything you need just ask Janice. She'll come sneaking back when I've left.'

When he had gone and Lesley heard the sound of the car engine fade in the distance, she went to the window and looked out. A velvety darkness had settled on the town since her arrival and now lights threaded the quayside and shone through the trees on the hill like adjacent stars. One distant light out at sea she took to be a buoy marking a rock formation. All round the coast she had noticed the outcrops of rock. She opened the window wide. It was not cold and the night air was scented from the azaleas by the front door. It was a heady perfume that aroused senses she had not experienced before, and she pushed the window down sharply, reluctant to indulge in sensuous fancies.

She thought of the dirty dishes she had left in the kitchen and the unknown Mrs Hatchet coming home late and finding them waiting for her. Aunt Celia's early training was too powerful to ignore, so she went back to the kitchen, washed up, put things away, then returned to unpack and soak in a hot scented bath before getting into bed.

She took a book to bed with her, a guide of Cornwall, but she couldn't concentrate—neither could she sleep; she was overtired and her mind too active. She tried to blot out the image of Neil Rodway as she had last seen him standing in the bedroom doorway saying good night. He was so tall his hair brushed the lintel of the door. When he had interviewed her she had found him distant and unapproachable—but here in his own home he had a more relaxed manner. She hoped they would get on better in future—after all, they had to work together, and for the sake of their patients there must not be any outward friction between them.

He had obviously been impressed by her new appearance, and this gave her a nice warm feeling of gratification; she was woman enough to like admiration. She made up her mind to take extra care with her make-up in the morning and to wear one of her new skirts.

She was just stretching out to switch off the bedside light when she heard a faint scratching on the door. She sat up and waited. The door partially opened and Jan's wide-eyed face appeared.

'You scared the life out of me!' exclaimed Lesley. 'I thought it was rats.'

'We don't have rats at Carn House, Mrs Hatchet wouldn't allow it.' Jan came in and then up to the bed. 'Has he gone?'

'If you mean your brother—yes, he has, back to the hospital. Oh, Jan, aren't you ashamed of yourself?'

The girl managed to look contrite and defiant at the same time. Lesley made room for her to sit beside her.

'He called me a thief,' Jan said crossly. 'I'm not a thief! I had to tell you that before I went to bed. I'm sorry it meant you had a bumpy ride in Dave's bus—a taxi would have been more comfortable but not so much fun. Was he furious?'

'He was certainly angry this evening, but I expect he'll have got over it by the morning. What made you do such a thing? If you so badly needed money I'm sure Dr Rodway would have lent it to you. Was it something you needed at school?'

'Goodness, no—Neil pays for everything there. It was for something much more important. It's Neil's birthday soon and I haven't any money for a present. I couldn't very well borrow from him to buy him a present with, could I?'

Lesley collapsed with laughter. 'Indeed not—much better to purloin it instead. So you're going to buy him a present with his own money. That's rich!'

'I'll pay him back,' said Jan quickly. 'My allowance from Daddy is due about now, though it's paid straight into the bank, and Neil controls it.' She sighed, her eyes roving around the room in an aimless fashion, but already her quicksilver mind was off on another tack. 'How do you like this room? Mummy had it done up the last time she was home.'

'It's the loveliest room I've slept in—it should give me sweet dreams tonight,' said Lesley. 'By the way, are you responsible for the primroses on the mantelpiece? That was a very nice thought.'

Jan squirmed with pleasure. 'I picked them in the lane for you. I always like to welcome our guests with flowers. Not that Vita Barry, though,' she added, her young brow darkening. 'If I'd known her better there'd have been thistles for her!'

Lesley laughed again. 'And what has this poor Vita Barry done to incur such displeasure?'

'Nothing. Just being herself—that was enough. Mrs Hatchet didn't like her either. Neil takes more notice of Mrs H than he does anyone else, so Vita won't be coming again. She didn't fit in anyway. I don't know what Neil saw in her. And she was here *three weeks*—it seemed more like three years! Thank goodness he lost her when he went to London recently. Did you meet her? Once seen, never forgotten—masses of red fuzzy hair and eyelashes a yard long!'

Lesley realised they were talking about the girl whom she had met with Neil on that first humiliating encounter at St Bede's Hospital, and then wondered why the news of her apparent eclipse should give her so much pleasure. She had a sudden impulse to hug young Janice, but resisted it, knowing it was born of an irrational emotion. Jan stood up and stretched.

'Oh, glory, I'm tired—I must get to bed. But I'm going down to raid the larder first—I'm starving!'

'Your brother said there was a ham Mrs Hatchet cooked yesterday, but we couldn't find it,' said Lesley.

'That should be in the meat safe in the back kitchen. Neil is an idiot—fancy not looking!' Swiftly and unexpectedly Jan bent down and gave Lesley a good night kiss. When she had gone Lesley lay back on her pillows, feeling a surge of warm affection for the girl sweep over her. She knew she and Jan were going to become close friends—but what about Neil? Would he also encourage friendliness? He had all the masculine traits she told herself she despised—arrogance, pride, a superiority; but to be fair he also had a robust sense of humour, a deep sense of family unity—and the bluest and most riveting eyes she had ever seen. And it was a visual image of those eyes she took with her into sleep.

All was quiet when she next awoke. She looked at the

bedside clock. Nine o'clock—she had slept the clock round! She jumped out of bed and ran to the upper hall. Leaning over the banisters, she could just catch the sound of movements from the kitchen, and the welcome aroma of coffee drifted up the stairs. She went back for her dressing-gown and slippers and hurried down the stairs.

The only person in the kitchen was a tall, spare woman with greying hair and a ramrod back. She looked at Lesley with cold grey eyes unnaturally enlarged by thick glasses.

'I—I overslept,' stammered Lesley. 'I'm Dr Colman. I'm sorry to be late. Have I missed Dr Rodway?'

'He left twenty minutes ago—he took his sister to school before going on to the surgery. He said I wasn't to disturb you. Breakfast is ready if you would like it now.'

'I'll dress first. I only want coffee—and perhaps toast,' Lesley added with haste, seeing the look of disapproval deepen on the other's face.

That Mrs Hatchet had no great opinion of the new boarder was apparent from her manner. On her part Lesley could not but think what a misfortune it was to have such a nose and chin with a name like Hatchet! She took the stairs two at a time; washed, dressed—no time for discreet make-up or choice of clothes—she grabbed the first to hand, a denim skirt Karen had given her for Christmas and a check shirt, made her bed, ran a comb through her hair, and was back in the kitchen within twenty minutes.

The table was set with cereals, marmalade and toast. Now a plate of bacon and egg was put before her. Though she hadn't believed she was hungry Lesley found the smell of bacon stimulated her appetite. She didn't leave much for the birds, and she didn't miss the look of triumph on Mrs Hatchet's face when she came to remove the plate.

'There is just one thing I'd like to get clear,' she said when Lesley was preparing to leave. 'If you must use my utensils would you please see that they're put back in their right place in future. I wasted several minutes this morning looking for my frying-pan.'

So that was what had offended her! Lesley made abject apologies, thinking that more diplomatic than making excuses, and Mrs Hatchet looked slightly mollified. She couldn't resist, however, handing Lesley her woollen hat as if it were a dirty rag she had found among her clean washing. 'And I believe this is yours. You left it behind the door. *That*'s where I hang my aprons!'

Lesley escaped. It was only when she was halfway down the drive she remembered she didn't know the location of the surgery. Reluctantly, she turned back.

Mrs Hatchet didn't hear the kitchen door open. She was leaning against the sink, gripping it for support, her head drooping. Instantly on the alert, Lesley hurried forward. 'Mrs Hatchet, is anything wrong?'

Immediately the older woman straightened her back, and Lesley saw then that she was unnaturally pale and her skin clammy. 'I'm perfectly all right,' she said impatiently.

'You don't look all right—'

'There's nothing wrong with me!' In fact the woman's voice was stronger and the colour was returning to her cheeks. Her eyes, behind her thick spectacles, glinted with annoyance. 'I came over a little dizzy, that's all. Too much excitement and rich food at my sister's yesterday. I wouldn't have gone all the way to Penzance if it hadn't been that it was her ruby wedding. I thought you'd gone—I was sure I heard the front door close.'

She said it in such a way as to suggest that Lesley had come sneaking back to spy on her.

Feeling about two inches tall, Lesley explained that she had forgotten to ask Dr Rodway directions to the surgery, and he had been in so much of a hurry last night he had forgotten to tell her. She listened meekly as Mrs Hatchet directed her in words a five-year-old would have understood.

But hurrying down the steep pathway a few minutes later she felt both physically and mentally renewed. The long sleep had done her a power of good, and she found the salty tang of the air invigorating. It was early April and the sun was growing in warmth. All the way down to the harbour road she had birdsong for company, and she suddenly felt carefree, with a sense of holiday freedom. For it did seem as if she was on holiday, a state of mind that only lasted until she reached the surgery door.

The surgery was a long low white building that had once been two coastguard cottages, Mrs Hatchet had told her. It was easily located right opposite the small jetty and next door to the Fishermen's Chapel. The garden was paved to make standing room for cars and there was a brass plate with Neil Rodway's name and qualifications, as well as those of his partner, Dr Christopher Watling. Lesley was surprised to see that as well as his medical degrees Dr Rodway also had a degree in surgery. James hadn't mentioned that, though now she remembered Karen saying something about Neil being interested in surgery. Still, an FRCS—something not likely to come her way for many years—and he had given it up to be a GP in an obscure Cornish resort. The man was mad!

She opened the door to the surgery to find herself in a large waiting area, carpeted and with upholstered benches and the usual medical posters on the walls. Five or six patients were already waiting. At the far end a section had been partitioned off—there was a counter with a hand-bell and a notice saying PLEASE RING. Behind a screen Lesley could hear the sound of typing, but it stopped when she rang the bell and a well-built middle-aged woman appeared.

'You have an appointment?' she asked.

'I'm Dr Colman.'

The woman blinked, caught unaware. She gave a momentary glance at Lesley's windswept hair, the anorak that had seen better days. 'I'm sorry, Doctor, I didn't realise. Dr Rodway said I was to show you straight in. Come this way, please.'

She led Lesley along a narrow passageway to a door marked with Neil's name. She knocked and held it open and Lesley went in.

There was a patient with Dr Rodway, a gaunt old man with sparse whiskers. Both looked round as she entered, then Neil came forward.

'Good morning. Mr Green, this is the new assistant I was telling you about. You won't mind if Dr Colman sits in at this appointment, will you?'

Mr Green gave Lesley a belligerent look from small but sharp black eyes. 'I do mind—I mind very much. I'm not going to be poked and prodded by some whey-faced young chit from London. I want a real doctor!'

Neil avoided Lesley's eyes. 'Dr Colman is a very competent medical practitioner. She was trained at my old hospital.'

'She's a woman, ain't she? I'm not letting any wimmin see me—not with my clothes off!'

This makes a nice change, thought Lesley. Here's one man who recognises me as a female.

Neil took her by the elbow and piloted her out of the room and into an empty surgery next door. 'Sorry about that,' he said, but he didn't look at all sorry. She thought she could detect a damning and sardonic twinkle in his eye. 'I had the same trouble with your predecessor. Old man Green has a thing about female doctors, and at his age I think it safer to humour him. Chris is out visiting the branch surgeries this morning, so make use of his room and I'll ask Miss Pearson to cream off some of my patients for you.'

Miss Pearson must have been given explicit instructions, Lesley considered wryly, as the three patients sent to her would not have taxed the abilities of newly-qualified medical students.

The first was a man going on a business trip to the West Indies who needed the necessary inoculations. The second patient required a medical for the purposes of a life insurance, and the last was a woman of late middle-age suffering from high blood pressure.

At first she was aggrieved at not seeing her usual doctor, but soon warmed to Lesley when she realised she was not inexperienced.

'I was put off lady doctors for a time,' she explained, as she watched Lesley replace the sphygmomanometer in its case. 'I didn't take to the one Dr Rodway had before you. The goings-on in that cottage she rented!'

Lesley recalled that Neil had referred to his first assistant as 'a right little sexpot'—and now her curiosity was aroused. But she only gave her patient a bland smile, checked with her record card that her blood pressure was no higher than on her last visit and wrote out a prescription for another supply of tablets.

The woman had just left when Neil came in. 'How have things been?'

'I won't suffer from overwork if all mornings are like this,' she said.

'They won't be. Wait until the season gets going, you'll soon notice the difference then.' He watched her with impassive blue eyes as she tidied the desk. 'You slept well last night.'

This quite innocuous statement caused her an overwhelming and inexplicable confusion. 'I did, but I wish you'd given me a call this morning. I didn't like being late my first day—'

'I did look in on you, but you were sleeping like an angel and I hadn't the heart to disturb you.' Again she could not be sure whether he was serious or just being flippant. She had the uncomfortable conviction he was shaking with inward laughter, and her resentment towards him flared anew.

'I actually called in to see about lunch arrangements,' he told her. 'I never bother with lunch myself, there are other things I'd rather use the time for—but that won't do for you. You need building up. If you'd like to go back to Carn House and have something with Mrs Hatchet I'll give you a lift up the hill. Jan has her lunch at school, of course. Alternatively, you could send out for a sandwich and join Miss Pearson in her office. She'd be pleased to make you coffee.'

Neither idea appealed to Lesley. The thought of lunching alone with the formidable Mrs Hatchet secretly appalled her, and equally she didn't like to intrude upon the receptionist. More than anything she wanted to be outdoors, within sight and sound of the sea.

The sun was warmer than she had expected, the sea was crested with small ripples, and again the air felt like silk against her skin. Across the road was a lock-up café doing a brisk trade in stuffed baked potatoes. Most of the customers seemed to be fishermen from the crab and lobster boats tied up to the jetty. Lesley went across. She couldn't manage a potato, but the sandwiches were freshly made, and she came away with one on a paper plate and a plastic beaker of coffee. Now to find somewhere to sit.

Threading her way through coils of rope, old crates, and the odd anchor and winch, she made her way to an empty bench at the far end of the jetty. Here she was in the full sun. Here, the only company was the screeching gulls, and here she could look out at an endless vista of blue water.

One particular gull, bolder or more hungry than its fellows, landed on the jetty rail within touching distance and fixed her with a menacing red eye. She threw him a piece of crust, and instantly found herself the centre of a whirling, screaming, diving cloud of seabirds. She stood up in order to take better aim and fed them the remainder of her sandwich. Feeding gulls was something she had not done since she was a child on holiday with her parents, and the memory came back on a wave of bittersweet longing. The breeze flipped her hair into her eyes and, laughing, she pushed it away. It was then she realised she was not alone.

A few yards away was a man with a sketch pad. He was a slight dark figure with a thin lined face and hooded dark eyes. He caught her eye and smiled faintly, his pencil working rapidly over the paper. Lesley had the uneasy feeling that he was sketching her, and though this didn't annoy her, she didn't like the idea of having her privacy violated.

She stood up and slung her bag over her shoulder. She had to pass him on her way back, and as she did so he said something which she did not catch, and she hurried on. A few steps farther on she looked back over her shoulder, then wished she hadn't—he was watching her with a brooding intensity. He looked dark enough to be a Celt, and she wondered if he was a local rather than a visitor.

But she quickly forgot him. It was just one of those chance encounters. She didn't expect to see him again.

CHAPTER FOUR

WHEN Lesley returned to the surgery after lunch Dr Watling was in his room, on the point of shrugging off his topcoat. He hung it on its peg, then came towards her with hand outstretched, smiling broadly. He was the same height and build as James, but a few years older, to judge by the amount of grey in his wavy brown hair.

'Welcome to Trevaise,' he said, pumping her hand up and down with vigour. 'Glad to have you aboard—things have been pretty dicey these past two weeks. Did they overwork you this morning?'

'I couldn't say that,' answered Lesley with a straight face.

'Mustn't wear you out. We've got to take care of a girl with your reputation.'

'My reputation?' She wondered what Neil had said about her.

'All those honours and prizes that have strewn the path of your student years.' He was teasing, but in the nicest possible way, so she didn't take offence as she would have had it been Neil. There was instant rapport between them and they were soon calling each other by their first names.

The phone interrupted them, and Dr Watling answered. 'Yes, Miss Pearson? Oh, put him through . . . what can I do for you, Neil? Yes, she's here. I'll tell her—' He replaced the receiver and grinned.

'That was Neil enquiring whether you were back from lunch. He's calling from Carn House to say he'll be along in five minutes. He wants you to accompany him on his rounds this afternoon. You see how quickly you're being broken in! The next thing you'll be doing house calls on your own!'

'I don't drive,' Lesley told him.

He stared for a bit, then spread his hands in a gesture which was to become very familiar to her in the weeks following. It could mean anything from 'So what?' to 'Hard luck!' He said; 'We'll find a way round that, don't worry.'

Lesley was waiting on the footpath before Neil arrived. It wasn't long before the powerful car purred into sight. Neil stopped only long enough to pick her up, then turned and headed back the way he had come. They rose swiftly up the winding hill road that skirted a pre-war housing estate and in no time were out in open countryside.

The large car ate up the miles. When, after leaving a belt of trees, they took a track across a wide stretch of moorland, Lesley began to wonder about the size of the practice. Surely it couldn't extend as far as this?—and they hadn't passed a house for miles. In fact the only building in sight was a derelict brick structure with a tall chimney on one side. She was puzzling what this could be when Neil said:

'Look over there—do you know what that is?' He didn't wait for an answer. 'It's one of Cornwall's famous engine houses. Once it contained an engine which provided the means of winding and pumping and ventilating the tin mines below. Some of the old engine houses have been renovated and turned into museums, some in the north are even working again—now powered by electricity—but most are like this, a ruined curiosity of another age.' He added, less seriously, 'Tread carefully over these moors, Dr Colman. They're riddled with old mineshafts—hidden traps for the unwary.'

She thought it unnecessary that he should take that tone—as if she were a child. 'Thank you for warning me,' she said stiffly. 'But you don't have to keep on with the "Dr Colman". My name's Lesley.'

'Is it? I thought it was Jane.' Again she had the uncomfortable conviction that he was laughing inwardly—she could tell by the gleam in his eyes. This was the first time she had met anybody who could infuriate her just by laughing, but she was determined not to let him see it.

He stopped the car. 'Would you like to explore?'

She was surprised; she thought they were out to make calls, not on a pleasure trip, but she followed him out of the car without question and stood beside him to stare out at the unfamiliar scene.

'I wouldn't call this beautiful country,' she said after a short silence. 'There's something about it even frightening. I can believe all those old tales of smugglers and footpads and quagmires!'

He laughed. 'That's Bodmin, or Dartmoor—nothing sinister about Barton Moor. For one thing it isn't vast enough. It isn't possible to get lost.'

'It isn't small either!' The moors stretched as far as the eye could see, an undulating sea of brown heather broken here and there by clumps of blazing gorse and outcrops of granite boulders and great mounds of blackthorn and bramble thickets. Neil pushed some of last year's heather aside so that Lesley could see the new growth of springing green shoots that would soon take over, transforming the moor with a carpet of pinks and mauves. A pair of birds appeared overhead, sweeping round the sky in wide spirals on broad rounded wings and giving plaintive mewing cries.

They watched the aerial courtship for several minutes, then Neil said, 'They're buzzards. They nest every year on the highest part of these moors. Well,' he smiled down at her, 'this has been a very pleasant little diversion, but now back to work. I have an appointment with my first patient at three o'clock.'

'A diversion?' she queried. 'This isn't part of your usual round, then?'

He laughed aloud at that. 'Good lord, I wish it was! It's a tonic to come up here. All this space, and the wind so fresh—a person can breathe here. I find it the next best thing to being at sea.'

It didn't affect Lesley like that. She found the moor wild and untamed and forbidding—but then, of course, she had spent all her life hemmed in by bricks and mortar. She wasn't used to this kind of freedom. She mused, looking once more at the buzzards as they soared effortlessly above. They, more than anything, were a symbol of how different life was here from what it had been in London.

'I've still got time before my appointment to show you our two branch surgeries,' said Neil as he turned the car into a lane leading off into the valley. 'We pass them on this road. Pringle and Polhearne, known commonly at the practice as the two P's.'

Lesley had never heard of branch practices, and Neil had to explain. When she discovered that one was held in a room at a sub-post-office, and the other was a converted chapel, she looked her disapproval. Neil gave her a condescending smile.

'My dear Dr Colman—I do beg your parden, *Lesley*—not all the inhabitants of these outlying hamlets possess cars, and public transport being virtually nonexistent, it's a question of the practice going to the patient, rather like the mountain going to Mahomet. When you take over the branch visits yourself you'll see how it works. I can assure you they're both very well run and very efficient.'

'There's only one problem,' said Lesley in a flat voice. 'I don't drive.'

There was a moment or two of stunned silence.

'My God! I didn't even think to ask you that. I assumed everybody over the age of seventeen could drive these days.'

'A common assumption,' she answered dryly.

Another fraught silence, then he said with a note of resignation, 'It's my own stupid fault. I should have made sure at the interview.'

'You mean you wouldn't have given me this job if you'd known I couldn't drive?'

'Surely it's pretty obvious to you that a doctor in a rural practice has to be able to drive!'

Lesley stared moodily out at the winding road. Did this mean an abrupt end to her temporary job—was it back to being a house officer with an eighty-hour week, broken nights and snatched meals? Trevaise suddenly seemed very desirable.

'I see this puts you in a difficulty,' she said earnestly. 'I shall leave as soon as it's possible—'

'Who said anything about you leaving? Good lord, woman, you've only just got here! We'll find a way out of this little difficulty, don't you fear. If necessary, Chris and I will do the branch surgeries between us, leaving you to manage the practice.'

He sounded now as if it were of no importance, yet a few minutes before his voice had grated with exasperation. Lesley believed he enjoyed putting her at a disadvantage, and notched up another small resentment against him.

They came to a village of whitewashed thatched-roofed cottages, all with trim gardens. It was as pretty as a picture on a calendar. Neil drew up before a pair of wrought-iron gates leading to the driveway of a large house. He cut the engine, then swivelled round to face her.

'Just a word before we go in to meet Mrs Fiske—or old Lady Fiske, as Chris calls her—you'll soon find out why. She's my only private patient and I inherited her with the practice. Try to overlook her feudal outlook, she belongs to a generation where one's social class was all-important. Look around you at these cottages—every one an artist's dream. They would have been snapped up years ago by wealthy incomers for holiday homes if it hadn't been for Mrs Fiske. They belong to the Fiske estate and most of the tenants are in her employ, or were until they retired. She won't let her cottages to anyone not Cornish born, which makes a welcome change for this part of the world. She has very few friends, but she hasn't a single enemy either, and that says much for her.'

'And what is her particular ailment?' Lesley had already met several 'Mrs Fiskes' in the Belvedere Nursing Home and on the whole hadn't been impressed.

'She broke her leg about six weeks ago through tripping over a footstool. I got her into hospital and set the leg myself. She was discharged two weeks ago and is making rather slow progress. Partly her own fault—she refused physiotherapy—said she wasn't going to be connected up to any contraptions at her time of life.' Neil smiled, but it was an indulgent smile, as if he secretly shared her point of view. 'I'm keeping an eye on her, though there were no complications. It was a nice clean break.'

Lesley stared at him in some bewilderment. '*You* set her leg! Is it usual for GPs to set fractures here?'

He looked at her steadily. 'I should have said I was wearing my other hat. You needn't look so disturbed —I'm quite capable of dealing with a simple fracture. Perhaps James mentioned that I do two sessions at the District Hospital as an orthopaedic surgeon?'

She swallowed. 'No—no, he didn't. I did see by your plate that you had an FRCS, but I thought you gave all that up to become a GP.'

There was a touch of resentment in his voice when he answered. 'You know, there's one trouble with you medics pigeonholed in your own compartments in our city hospitals—you haven't got a clue as to what's going on in country practices, have you? Just because we're GPs it doesn't mean we go about with straws in our hair and apply leeches to our patients. Most GPs have specialised in another branch of medicine. Chris, for instance, has a diploma in Public Health. I could show you some group practices that are microcosms of any general hospital. When my grandmother died and left Carn House to me and at the same time I learnt that old Dr Williams was selling up and retiring, I thought the opportunity too good to miss. I'd spent all my school holidays in Trevaise—now I had the chance to make it my home, so I bade farewell to St Bede's and bought the practice. I've enlarged it since, built it up and added the branch surgeries, but I didn't want to give up surgery entirely and as I'd specialised in orthopaedics I arranged to do two sessions a week at the local hospital. I hope that will banish any idea that I ran away from work of more importance to bury myself down here.'

Lesley realised she had misjudged him; she realised too that her attitude could be seen as patronising. To be quite honest, she had nursed a hidden conviction that she, an aspiring surgeon with primary FRCS on the horizon, had more to offer the practice than the practice had to offer her. She felt humbled—and it showed on her face. She felt something even more disconcerting when Neil unexpectedly placed his hand over hers.

'Cheer up,' he said. 'I didn't mean to bawl you out —you weren't to know. Now prove I'm forgiven by hopping out and opening the gates for me.'

Lesley was glad of this chance for action. To sit in the car with him while her heart pounded against her ribs, anxious in case he should hear it—though common sense told her that was a physical impossibility—still, something could betray her agitation. And what had brought it on? Not the touch of his hand, surely. It was only a friendly gesture meant to put her at her ease—but never before had she felt this quickening of the senses, and it brought her face to face with her own vulnerability. It seemed ironic that the first man to arouse her dormant sensuality was this man who in every other way infuriated her.

She got back into the car and sat silent and thoughtful as they nosed up the long narrow drive, then at the sudden sight of a field of daffodils she gave an exclamation of delight.

'I've never seen anything like that before! It looks like a carpet of gold!'

Neil nodded. 'Yes, it's certainly a picture at this time of year. They're wild daffodils—been growing in that meadow for as long as anyone around here can remember, and for that reason Mrs Fiske won't allow that piece of land to be ploughed up or cultivated. Good for her!'

They stopped outside a large stone mansion, a solid-looking residence built more to withstand the westerly gales than with an eye to elegance, but today, bathed in the pale spring sunshine, it had a certain austere beauty. The door was opened to them by the housekeeper, a young woman in her thirties, who showed them to a room on the ground floor where an elderly woman reclined on a sofa with her leg on a cushion.

Lesley, who had got the idea from what Neil had said that Mrs Fiske was another Mrs Hatchet, was surprised to see she was a small, even frail old lady, but when a pair of sharp green eyes suddenly focused on her with a glacier stare, she realised he hadn't been fabricating.

Mrs Fiske said, 'What extraordinary-coloured hair! Is it natural?' Her voice rose on a note of intimidation, making Lesley conscious of her windswept appearance —she was certainly not Mrs Fiske's idea of a lady doctor.

But Mrs Fiske could also be gracious. 'You're looking very pale, my dear,' she said. 'One must expect that, living in London, so you should take the opportunity to be out of doors while you can. Yvonne will show you the way to my daffodil meadow. You may pick as many blooms as you like.'

It sounded like a generous gesture, but it was actually a command. Lesley understood: Mrs Fiske wanted to be alone with the doctor of her choice.

She was shown out through a side door leading on to a path that went straight to the meadow. The daffodils were so thick on the ground she couldn't avoid trampling some of them down. It didn't take her long to pick an armful. They were smaller and shorter than the cultivated varieties, but lovely for all that. She buried her nose in them, drinking in their rare fragrance, stifling for a moment the conflicting doubts that had beset her since arriving at Trevaise.

Hearing a twig snap, she turned, thinking it was Neil—but it was not Neil; it was a slight, dark man who came towards her walking with a limp only discernible to the practised eye. She recognised the man with the sketchbook on the jetty that morning, and he recognised her—she could tell that by the way his thin lips twisted into a smile of greeting.

'This morning you were surrounded by a host of seagulls—now I find you buried beneath daffodils. I think I prefer the flowers,' he said.

He was shorter than she, but that didn't seem to affect him as it did some men who had to look up to her. His smile broadened.

'I see you've been helping yourself. Nobody would dare attempt that without my aunt's permission. It's a rare honour—I wonder what your influence is?'

Lesley explained her position, and thought he looked momentarily displeased.

'So you're Dr Rodway's new assistant. Well, well—when I first saw you I imagined you many things, but not a doctor.'

'What, then?' she queried.

'A visitor, perhaps. You were taking such delight in feeding seagulls—I could say, a childlike delight. That ruled out you being a model. I've met few childlike models.'

She wondered if his cynicism had anything to do with his limp. He looked like a man who had suffered. Then he shook her composure by saying:

'Would you let me paint you? I have the pencil sketch I did of you, but it doesn't do you justice. As soon as I clapped eyes on you I knew I had to paint you. A face like yours is a chance in a lifetime.'

Selfconsciously Lesley put her hands to her cheeks and then to her hair. 'But why me? I must look an awful mess—I've been on the moors—'

'But you wouldn't look a mess if you sat for me by appointment—I'd arrange things differently,' he said, humouring her.

She didn't like this infringement of her privacy and she began to make excuses. 'I wouldn't have the time to sit for a portrait—and in any case, I'm not beautiful.'

That annoyed him. 'Beauty—what do you mean by beauty? If it's just chocolate-box prettiness it can be applied—that's no problem. It's the basic structure of your face I'm interested in—it's a gift for any artist.' His dark hooded eyes held a feverish intensity. 'I've returned to Trevaise as I do every summer to stay with my aunt and to have a break from the world of lovely women constantly clamouring for attention—and what do I find my first day here? Someone who's filled me with such excitement as I haven't known for years. Forgive me,' he said suddenly, 'my fervour has run away with me and I think I've offended you.'

Lesley wasn't offended so much as embarrassed. She wasn't used to strange men speaking with such candour and wasn't sure whether to take him seriously or not. At the same time she realised she had met someone who didn't make her feel gawky and clumsy, and for that reason alone she might agree to his request. But she was still too cautious to say yes straight away.

'We haven't even been introduced yet,' she said, trying to make a joke of it.

'We have—we introduced ourselves. My name is Colin Bucknall—' he paused as if waiting for some reaction, and when none came from her a certain wryness came into his expression. 'And you—?'

'Colman—Lesley Colman.'

'Lesley—I like that, it suits you. May I call you Lesley?'

It was refreshing to be asked. He treated her with a touch of deference which seemed oddly old-fashioned. From the direction of the house came the blare of a car's hooter.

Colin raised his eyebrows. 'Your colleague appears to be impatient.'

'My boss, actually,' she corrected him. She turned and walked back towards the house, conscious that he was following her. Neil greeted her with a scowl when he saw that she was not alone.

The two men nodded curtly to each other, and seeing the look that passed between them Lesley was aware of a mutual antipathy.

She said, 'I'm sorry I've kept you. I've been busy—look!'

'Very nice.' Neil glared sourly at the daffodils, then opened the car door for her. Before getting in himself he said to Colin, 'Your aunt is progressing quite satisfactorily, but she needs to build up her leg muscles. Pity she doesn't take more exercise. Perhaps you could persuade her to try walking more?'

'Have you been able to persuade her to have physiotherapy treatment?'

'No.'

Colin smiled meaningly. 'Well then—'

Neil slammed the car door shut. The engine throbbed into life and with some unnecessary revving they roared off down the drive.

'I can't stand that fellow,' he said savagely. 'Every time I see a reproduction of one of his pictures I feel like chucking the damn thing out of the window!'

Something went click in Lesley's memory. Colin Bucknall—of course, she remembered the name now. She had seen a preview of some of his work on television. He was becoming known as a Cornish seascape artist, but he had also painted some portraits of women, and without exception they were all tall, willowy and beautiful—so much so that they were known as the 'Bucknall Girls'. And he had asked *her* to sit for him? The inferiority complex she had about her height suddenly seemed meaningless. Then, looking up, she saw Neil watching her in the driving mirror, and didn't know that excitement had coloured her cheeks and added an extra lustre to her eyes.

'You look pleased with yourself,' he said shortly.

She told him that Colin wanted to paint her, and was surprised how this affected him. His face went dark with anger. 'I wouldn't sit for him during surgery hours,' she pointed out.

But that wasn't what was worrying him. 'I hope to God you'd have more sense than to sit for him any old hour.' His voice was bitter. 'The blighter didn't take long to get round you!'

His assumption angered her in turn. 'What a beastly thing to suggest! There's no question of him getting round me!'

'No? *I* wouldn't trust him further than I could see him. And what are you trying to prove? When I first met you you wanted to be a surgeon. Now it seems you're hankering to be an artist's model!'

His unjust accusation stung her to tears. As she struggled for self-control she realised that a small thing like Colin asking her to pose for him could not have sparked off such irrational anger. There must be some other deep-rooted cause for Neil's dislike of the other man. Something must have happened between them in the past which had left a legacy of hate.

Then, realising that he might have overreacted, Neil gave her a quizzical grin—like a small boy trying to make amends after a fit of tantrums. 'He's a bally old woman too—rushes off to a warmer climate as soon as the first leaves begin to fall. Says the cold weather is bad for his constitution!'

It would have been funny if it hadn't been so ludicrous. She didn't know how to take him—raving at her one minute, now chaffing her.

'I would have thought, as a medical man, you would have shown more sympathy towards him,' she said primly. 'Have you noticed his limp? I wondered if he'd been in an accident?'

Neil went white under his tan and didn't answer at first. Then gruffly he said, 'He *was* in an accident, out East, some years ago, and allowed some unqualified quack to have a go setting a badly fractured ankle. I've offered to put it right for him, it's an easy enough job, but he won't let me near him—or any surgeon, come to that. Now can we please let the subject of Colin Bucknall drop? I've got more important things on my mind.'

Lesley lapsed into thought. Neil had revealed more by what he had not said rather than by what he had. She felt that the accident was an important clue to their shared dislike. And why had Neil offered to operate on a man he distrusted, to help him in that way? Because of some hidden guilt, or was it just professional pride? Wearily she brushed all assumptions aside. She was going to be in Trevaise for so short a time, why let someone else's quarrel worry her?

Neil didn't speak again until they stopped outside a humble-looking cottage. Remembering the splendour of Mrs Fiske's home and then comparing it with this tumbledown place brought home to Lesley the contrasts in the practice. Not that it made any difference to Neil; he treated all his patients alike.

Bert Gooley was an eighty-five-year-old ex-sailor suffering from an ulcerated leg. Lesley drew her breath in sharply as Neil removed the dressing. The leg was inflamed and swollen, and the ulcer had infected a large part of the shin. She marvelled with what gentleness Neil dealt with the old man, how tenderly he applied a fresh dressing.

'That's all for today,' he said, as he straightened up. 'How did you come to break it open this time, Bert? Stumbled into the table again? You really must take more water with your medicine!' He lifted a nearly empty bottle of whisky from the sideboard and held it against the light. 'Only two doses left, I see. I'd better let you have another bottle. I'll send it round with Nurse, tomorrow.'

Once outside Lesley could not contain herself any longer. 'Is it usual in Trevaise to prescribe spirits on the National Health?' she demanded sarcastically.

'Who said anything about the National Health.'

'You mean—*you* provide it? That makes it worse! Surely the money would be better spent on cleaning materials or employing somebody to give that cottage a thorough spring-clean. It's absolutely filthy!'

Neil placed himself in front of her and stared at her with eyes like two narrow blue slits. 'Have you got a bottle of carbolic under your rib-cage in place of a heart?' he demanded in a steely voice. 'If anybody deserves a few drinks at his time of life old Bert does. He spent three years in a Japanese prisoner-of-war camp —and that's where he first contracted that tropical ulcer.

It's never completely cleared up, and it won't do so now, the blood supply to his legs is too poor. He's in constant pain and discomfort, and if a small drink helps him get through the day, I say good luck to him. All I can say is, *Dr* Colman,' and he stressed this last word, 'it's a pity you didn't take a course in humanities along with all your other credits, it might have taught you some compassion!'

He strode off, leaving her speechless and staring after him with welling eyes. Angrily she brushed away the tears, not wanting him to see such weakness. She was angry with herself too for giving him the impression that she was insensitive to the old man's suffering. She ran after him to tell him this, but he too had had time to think and was obviously sorry for his latest outburst.

Before she could speak he said in a more temperate voice, 'I take back what I just said—I didn't mean it. It's just that your prissiness got up my nose. I haven't got any time for prudery, it's usually the last resort of someone either very narrowed-minded or uncharitable or both. I don't believe you're either narrow-minded or uncharitable—just rather tactless.'

He smiled; he could be very charming when he liked. 'Only one more call, then back to Carn House and a very welcome cup of tea before evening surgery. You've had a long day,' he conceded. 'We did push you in the deep end. I think you've done us proud.'

If he thought by those few kind words he could undo the hurt he had inflicted, he was wrong. But he seemed unaware of Lesley's seething emotions as he headed the car towards the council estate. She slumped in the seat beside him, staring unseeingly out of the window. How long would it be before she could laugh at the idea of having a bottle of carbolic instead of a heart?

CHAPTER FIVE

In spite of its many traumatic moments that first day at Trevaise was to prove an easy one for Lesley as far as work was concerned. In the days that followed she was to spend many hours at the surgery getting to know her patients—not that she minded that. She enjoyed being occupied, and though many of the cases were routine complaints there was the occasional problem that stretched her expertise to its limits. It was a source of satisfaction to her when she was able to work things out for herself and not have to bother Neil or Chris for advice.

As she wrote in her first letter to Karen:

. . . 'If I'd taken up the secretarial work my aunt wanted and had made mistakes in my typing or book-keeping I could have cost the firm money. But if I make a mistake here, it could cost somebody their life.'

After three weeks in Trevaise she was fitter than at any time in her life and could look back with a smile at that first breathless climb up to Carn House. Now she could do it with ease, and even her house calls to the Woodside Estate, a round trip of three miles, seemed no effort. Better still, the open air and fresh salty winds had given a pale golden glow to her skin, so that the irascible Mr Green could no longer call her a whey-faced chit. But she could still not overcome his mistrust of women doctors.

It was a different case with Bert Gooley. He welcomed her visits, and not only because she usually took him some small gift. The first cost her nothing, a bunch of primroses she had picked on her way up thinking they would help liven up the drab living-room. His delight had been touching.

'It's years since I bin able to go out primrosing,' he said, his voice husky with emotion. 'I used to pick 'em for my mother on Mothering Sunday, bless 'er 'eart.' He took a sniff. 'My, ain't they 'andsome!'

Another time she took him an ounce of tobacco—she had noticed his empty pouch. She didn't tell Neil and she hoped old Bert wouldn't tell on her either, but for her own peace of mind she had to square her conscience. Neil had been right about the whisky.

She took it in turns with Moira Howard, the district nurse, to dress Bert's leg. She had taken to Moira on their first meeting. Moira was a pleasant, smiling girl with brown curly hair and hazel eyes, not exactly pretty but wholesome-looking and dependable. She was a familiar figure in Trevaise, driving round its lanes in her Mini in her smart blue uniform. Often she would overtake Lesley and give her a lift back to the surgery. She had even offered Lesley the loan of her car if she decided to take driving lessons and though tempted by her generosity, Lesley refused. She wanted to repay Karen before taking on other expenses.

She wrote several times to Karen in her first weeks, she had so much to relate. She thought about writing a letter to her aunt, but wrote to the Matron of the Belvedere instead. To her aunt she sent picture postcards, knowing she would take a childlike interest in looking at them.

By now she was well acquainted with Fran, Chris Watling's wife. At first she was slightly put off by her brittle manner, until she realised it masked a highly-strung disposition. Fran lived freely off her nerves and had so much pent-up energy that she couldn't sit still a minute. She was the complete antithesis of Chris, sallow where he was florid, diminutive where he was expansive. They were the perfect foil for each other.

They lived in a pretty house called Cliff Cottage—a misnomer, as it was too modern and roomy to be classed as a cottage, but it had deep eaves and gable windows and gave that effect. It overlooked Trevaise Cove, and was built on a ledge of a cliff. All the land belonging to it, which wasn't much, was in the front—cliffs rose like a granite wall behind, and the first time Lesley saw it she thought how cosy it looked tucked in a fold in the promontory, but its real advantages were only visible from inside. Then, sitting in a wide window was like being on the prow of a ship, for there was nothing in front but the seas crashing against the rocks below.

Lesley often wished she could spend more time with Fran, especially after Jan left to spend her Easter holidays with friends in St Ives. The house seemed dead without her and made Lesley realise how much she had come to rely on her bright and lively presence for company. She found that evenings at Carn House were the hardest to get through, when time seemed to go by in reverse. Breakfast was a hasty, informal affair, but dinner served formally in the dining-room was like a penance. The room itself was oppressive enough, with a lot of dark panelling and north-facing windows, and Mrs Hatchet's presence even more so. Neil insisted she ate with them—he wouldn't tolerate any old-fashioned notions of servants knowing their place, and Mrs Hatchet showed her disapproval by sitting tight-lipped throughout the meal, giving the impression that she was only waiting for the first opportunity to escape. Lesley, who had no small talk, hardly contributed to the conversation; they couldn't talk shop in front of the housekeeper, which left Neil to carry the brunt. After one or two subjects had died for want of stimulation he usually buried his face in a yachting magazine or something similar. Then the only sound in the room was the scrape of knives and forks on china and the steady, solemn tick of the grandfather clock.

It wasn't until Mrs Hatchet dropped a chance remark one day that Lesley realised the evening ritual was on her behalf. Before her coming Jan had had all her meals in the kitchen, and Neil's supper, on a tray, was taken to him in his study. This information only added to Lesley's wretchedness, and she wondered how she could get round the problem. Feeling even more that she was in the way, she usually escaped up to her own room after dinner. There she did her little bit of washing and hung it to dry in the bathroom, then she either wrote to Karen or read—usually textbooks.

She could have stayed downstairs and watched television, but now that Janice had gone nobody else seemed interested in it. Mrs Hatchet busied herself in the kitchen while she listened to her radio, and Neil usually went out. Sometimes he was called out to a patient, and it was then Lesley felt she wasn't pulling her weight because she couldn't take a turn at being on call, but often he went out purely for pleasure. She could always tell. Those evenings he bounded up the stairs two at a time, humming between his teeth, and came down again in casual clothes, usually shouting instructions to Mrs Hatchet over his shoulder as he made for the door. 'I'm not taking my keys with me, Mrs H, so don't lock me out. And please will you leave me a glass of milk and a sandwich for when I get back.' Or more often, 'Don't bother about a tray tonight, Mrs H. I'll have something at the Club.'

That club caused Lesley much conjecture. She pictured it as a place of soft lights and sweet music, exotic food and well-groomed female company. Her most restless nights were entirely due to wondering about that club.

Sometimes she wished Neil would spend more time at home, but only for Mrs Hatchet's benefit, she was quick to tell herself. She was worried that there was something amiss with the housekeeper. She didn't look well, and sometimes she grabbed hold of a chair or a shelf as if to steady herself. The only time Lesley tried to ask her about it, apart from that first morning, she was met with such a sharp rebuke she had been reluctant to say anything since. In any case, it was Neil's job to do so.

Sometimes, sitting in her room at twilight watching the first stars beginning to shine through the thin clouds, Lesley would feel a sense of sadness steal over her. She couldn't tell why, except that twilight had always seemed to her the saddest part of the day. It wasn't that she was discontented. In spite of her fears about coming to Trevaise she had not once regretted it; she felt a peace of mind she had never known at the hospital. There she had been too rushed—the pressures too great. Perhaps that was what had accounted for what Neil had called her uptightness. Only in one respect had she exchanged one kind of tension for another—and that was due to Neil.

She couldn't say why he had such an effect on her. He was like a force that attracted and repelled her at the same time, and he had a powerful animal magnetism that set her own responses quivering. As soon as he came too near her she felt so ill at ease that she was at once on the defensive, and what made it worse was that he sensed her antagonism. She was sometimes aware that he was watching her as if trying to account for the reason for her discomfiture, but whenever she caught his eye he gave her a look so bland and at the same time so searching that it was she who looked away in confusion. For this reason alone it was a relief to hear the door close behind him, but she paid for it in loneliness. It struck her as ironic that now she had the time and the inclination to make friends, few were available to her. There was Moira and Fran, both of whose friendship she would have valued, but Moira looked after an invalid mother when off duty and Fran had Chris, while Lesley herself was too reserved to make the first move.

And what about Colin Bucknall? She sometimes gave him a passing thought—always with some annoyance. She hadn't seen or heard of him since that day at High Moors—so much for his eagerness to paint her! Obviously a case of out of sight, out of mind. She wished she could feel like that about Neil, but she shrank from analysing her thoughts too deeply where he was concerned.

Curiosity about his private life sometimes got the better of her. Karen had said he attracted girls like bees round a honey-pot, but she hadn't seen any evidence of that so far. Then one night, when she was sitting up later than usual, something happened to give her complacency a sharp jolt.

It was a warm night and there was a full moon. Lesley sat at the open bedroom window drinking in the night scents from the garden below and listening to the far-away calls of the curlews. A skeletal tree whitened by moonshine threw a long dark shadow across the lawn and across this shadow, she now saw walking, the figures of a man and a girl. There was no mistaking who the man was, his height and the way he held his head showed her it was Neil. The girl was much shorter than he and standing very close. She laughed prettily, and the resonant tones of Neil's voice as he answered her seemed to fill the silence. He bent his head demandingly, the girl flung her arms round his neck and they were embracing with an undisguised passion.

Lesley could watch no longer. She closed the window softly, drew the curtains and going to her bed sat on it with hands locked together to stop them trembling. She knew by the thudding of her heart, by the sudden unbearabale pain that seemed to clutch her by the throat, that she was in the throes of a bitter jealousy. And if she was jealous at seeing Neil with another woman it could only mean one thing. Dry-eyed, she lay across her bed trying to face this new dilemma. It seemed incredible to her that she could have fallen in love with this man who had aroused such antipathy in her.

Her determination to make him aware of her as a woman, the words she had uttered to herself that awful occasion in the staff canteen, were now but a hollow mockery. She rolled over on to her face and gave way to racking sobs—and then was ashamed for being so weak-minded. She would never have believed she could have acted like this—like a lovesick girl. After she had splashed her face with cold water she felt better, but it took a night of restless introspection before she came to a decision. She would have to leave Carn House at the first opportunity.

At breakfast the next morning Neil explained that he had left his car overnight at the garage to have the tyres changed and so wouldn't be able to give her a lift to the surgery. She had wondered, in a dull kind of way, during her night of misery, why she hadn't heard the Audi's engine. This was why. 'I don't mind walking,' she said, trying to put some life in her voice.

'I'll walk with you, then.' She hadn't bargained on that. Fate was determined to prolong her torture.

She couldn't think straight with him walking beside her, and yet she found silence even more unnerving. Neil was the one who usually did all the talking, but this morning he seemed preoccupied. 'Jan should be home soon,' she said at last in desperation.

'Sunday, I hope. Then Mrs H is off for a few days.'

This gave her the opening she had been wanting for sometime.

'I'm concerned about her. I wanted to have a word with you about her condition—'

'Who, Jan's?' His words cut across hers in surprise.

'No! Mrs Hatchet's. I should have told you before —my first morning here I found her on the point of collapse. She felt very clammy and was feeling dizzy, but she refused to be examined and wouldn't even discuss it with me. Several times since I've suspected her of having vertigo. As she won't listen to me, I thought perhaps a word from you—'

She looked at him from under her thick lashes. He was frowning, his lips pursed. 'Right, I'll have a word with her,' he said thoughtfully. 'Though I don't suppose there's anything serious the matter. She's very touchy about her health, likes to think she's as fit as a fiddle—I suppose we all do. I have noticed a tendency to deafness lately, but I put that down to her age. Anyway, thanks for telling me and for showing such concern.'

He relapsed into his former preoccupation, though Lesley had the feeling that at times he stole sidelong serious glances at her. Once her attention wandered and she tripped on the steep cobbled path. At once his hand was on her elbow, steadying her. 'Whoa there!' he said. 'Can't have you taking another header!'

It was the word header that got her, bringing back as it did an image of herself sprawling in the hospital corridor, her foot entwined with his. His touch had sent an electric shock of awareness coursing through the whole of her body, and this too was the reason she drew her arm away and said stiffly, 'Thank you, but I'm in no danger of coming to grief. I've got myself well in hand.'

After that they walked with about three feet of daylight between them.

Lesley didn't see Neil again that morning. She had a busy surgery and he was due at the hospital for his morning session in the operating theatre. That afternoon she had several calls to make on the Woodside Estate, and afterwards, walking back to the surgery, she passed Cliff Cottage.

Fran had taken advantage of the fine spring afternoon to lift the daffodils that had finished flowering, piling them up in the wheelbarrow alongside. She straightened her aching back just as Lesley came into sight, walking with that long-legged stride that was so charactertistic. Fran was able to watch her, herself unseen, hidden by the fresh green growth of the lilac hedge, and thought how much Lesley had improved in appearance since their first meeting nearly a month before.

Her skin glowed with a golden radiance that looked striking against her ash-blonde hair and clear brown eyes. Lesley was one of those women, Fran decided, whose beauty grew with acquaintanceship. At first sight she had thought her too lanky and too thin, now she was filled with admiration for her erect carriage and narrow hips. Her eyes, too, looked as if they were lit up from within. Fran popped her head over the hedge and said, 'You look too disgustingly healthy by far.'

Lesley jumped. 'Why are you hiding there?'

'I'm not hiding, I'm gardening, and I'm just knocking off for a cuppa. Would you join me?'

Lesley consulted her watch. 'I've got half an hour and I'm dying for a cup of tea.'

The kitchen of Cliff Cottage was the most important room of the house. It faced the sea, and here Fran and Chris took most of their meals. Lesley was made to sit while Fran put the kettle on and got out the tea things. 'You just stay put,' she ordered. 'It's quite a trek up to the Estate and back, so rest while you can.'

Lesley didn't need telling twice. She loved Fran's kitchen—though she sometimes wondered whether conservatory would not have described it better, for wherever there was space to spare, there was a pot plant. Fran's mania for gardening had followed her indoors. And gardening wasn't her only skill. She was also clever with her needle and a superb cook. 'About the only thing I can't do,' she had said on one bitter occasion to Lesley, 'is to produce a baby.' It was the only time she referred to her childlessness.

Freshly baked scones, homemade jam and clotted cream appeared with the tea. Lesley had eaten more cream in the past month than in all the years before, but it hadn't made any noticeable difference to her figure.

Fran studied her scone with a critical eye before taking a bite. 'How's the old dragon up at Carn House?' she asked.

'Do you mean Mrs Hatchet!'

'I certainly don't mean Neil! Yes, Mrs Hatchet. Doesn't she go behind you all the time with her carpet-sweeper picking up the crumbs?'

Lesley surprised herself by jumping so quickly to the housekeeper's defence. 'She certainly does not! She's houseproud, but I've known worse.' Lesley's thoughts went back to Aunt Celia's régime. 'And I tell you another thing—when the primroses Jan had picked for my bedroom all died she replaced them with some violets. I thought that was very revealing, but she didn't like it when I tried to thank her.'

Fran stared at her with level grey eyes. 'You must have tamed her—unless it's her natural reverence for all medical practitioners. She certainly didn't put violets in that room when Vita Barry stayed there—deadly nightshade if she'd thought of it, no doubt!'

An image of the girl with red hair and the greenish-grey eyes floated before Lesley's eyes. She blinked it away and looked thoughtfully down at her cup. Another image came to torment her—a girl bathed in moonlight, a silhouette against a moon-whitened tree. There had been no telling the colour of *her* hair or eyes.

'Mind you, none of us cottoned on to her,' Fran was saying. 'It amazed us what Neil saw in her, she wasn't his type at all. She didn't last long. She didn't pass the test.'

'Test?' Lesley looked up.

There was a malicious glint in Fran's eyes. 'I was saying Vita didn't pass the test. She didn't take to Neil's mistress—no way would she share him.'

Lesley's mouth went dry. Again she thought of the mystery girl in the moonlight. 'Mistress?' To her own ears her voice sounded like a croak.

Fran couldn't hide her amusement. 'Hasn't Neil told you about the great love of his life?'

'He has not! And I wouldn't encourage such a discussion if he attempted to.'

Fran started to laugh, her narrow shoulders shaking uncontrollably. 'Oh, Lesley, you're priceless—your voice! "I wouldn't encourage such a discussion if he attempted to,"' she mimicked in a fair imitation of Lesley's tone. 'And your expression! It looked as if it had been set in concrete. Stay there—I'll get a photo of her.'

There was no point in Fran telling her to stay, she had no alternative, though she would have escaped if she could. She didn't want to see a likeness of the most important woman in Neil's life. She didn't want Fran to see her face as she was made to look at it, she knew she couldn't keep up this façade much longer.

Fran returned holding a framed picture. She placed it face up on the table. 'Look!'

Lesley looked—only she knew the effort it cost her—then became speechless.

'Well?' said Fran.

'It's—it's a *boat!*'

'A boat!' retorted Fran scathingly. 'It's not just a boat—it's a beautiful Bermudan-rigged sloop. Look at those lines—as slender as a racing yacht. Yes, she has speed, and room too—six berths. We had a lovely holiday in the Scilly Isles on her last year. That's when Chris took this photograph—from the dinghy. You can just see Neil at the wheel.'

Lesley looked long at the picture of the white yacht, its sails full of wind, the sea creaming at its bow, the translucent green water a wide backdrop. She could just make out the figure of a man in the cockpit, and only knew it was Neil because of his corn-gold hair. 'I didn't know,' she said simply.

'I'm surprised Neil didn't tell you. Didn't you wonder where he got to most evenings?'

'I thought he was at a club. I thought he was going out to enjoy himself.'

'So he was. Neil's idea of enjoyment is plunging in a twenty-foot trough during a storm at sea, or in winter in driving rain dressed in oilskins scraping and cleaning and painting its bottom with anti-fouling when it's up on stocks. She's in dry-dock now, and that's where Neil goes in his free time, getting her ready for the season. He's hoping to launch her in a week or two. Now do you understand about Vita Barry? She couldn't bear to be neglected, and any woman who wants Neil will have to learn to share him with his yacht *Seawife*. Aptly named, don't you think?'

Fran began to laugh again. 'You took the word mistress literally! Oh, you should have seen yourself, sitting there all prissy showing your disapproval!'

The word prissy opened up fresh wounds. Lesley tried to smile, tried to disguise her hurt. 'I should have guessed. I suppose club means the Trevaise Yacht Club, I've passed it often enough. And Jan said something about sailing—not *Seawife*, surely?'

'No. But it won't be long, she crews for Neil already. She's got her own little sailing dinghy Neil bought her, and he taught her to sail just as old Bert Gooley taught him when he was a child.'

So that accounted for the bottles of whisky. Lesley thought the closeness between them was more than a doctor-patient relationship. With some reluctance she handed the photograph back to Fran. The world of boats was a closed shop as far as she was concerned.

'You'll be joining us for some sailing trips this summer,' said Fran lightly. 'There are some lovely creeks around here to explore—'

'Not me,' put in Lesley quickly, wanting to put Fran

right on that score at once. 'I get seasick just crossing on the Woolwich Ferry!'

Fran thought it a facetious remark not worth acknowledging. She went on as if Lesley hadn't interrupted. 'I'm glad you've come to live in Trevaise—I don't make friends easily, I'm too fond of saying what I think, and that doesn't make for a harmonious relationship. You're a marvel to put up with me.'

'As long as you can put up with yourself!' Lesley was practising her best bedside manner. It was a joke between them. She pushed back her chair. 'I must go now.'

'No, wait!' There was a note of urgency in Fran's voice. She grasped Lesley's wrist, her thin hand brown against Lesley's much paler skin. 'I've been wanting to say this to you and haven't known how to put it. I—I suppose you wouldn't consider leaving Carn House and moving in with us?'

Lesley sat down again rather sharply. 'It's too much of a coincidence, she told herself; this was preordained. 'Does Chris know about this?' she asked, bewildered.

'Yes, we've talked it over. As a matter of fact I wanted him to sound you out first, but he said it was my idea and I must see it through myself. Didn't you think it strange when I spoke about Mrs Hatchet the way I did? I was trying to make an opening then.'

The two girls looked earnestly at each other, the width of the table between them. 'I do want to leave Carn House,' Lesley admitted, though nothing would have induced her to give the true reason. 'I do feel in the way there, and Mrs Hatchet won't let me help her. Neil won't allow me to pay anything towards my keep—won't even discuss it with me. It's very embarrassing.'

'You can help me all you like,' said Fran quickly. 'And

I'll charge you what you were paying at the hostel, if that makes you feel any better.'

'You won't make any profit out of that,' Lesley scoffed.

'I don't want to make a profit, I just want your company. I get very lonely here at times—you can see there are no neighbours, and when I'm lonely I get very depressed, which is hard on poor old Chris. We've got a very attractive spare room. It's yours if you only say the word.'

The offer was too tempting to resist. Dreams of a small cottage of her own faded from Lesley's mind. It would have been out of her reach, anyway; summer lets in Trevaise were around a hundred pounds a week. Fran wanted her company—*she* wanted to escape from Carn House, so this seemed the perfect solution.

Then when she saw the spare bedroom she knew it was to be. It was such a pretty room, its predominant colour blue, and she would be able to lie in bed and listen to the sea.

Fran could tell she had won her case. 'I'm glad this room is going to be used at last.' She spoke quietly. 'It's crying out for an occupant. I think there's nothing sadder than an unused room.' Her eyes turned bleak with despair. 'I had hoped to make it into a nursery, but it wasn't to be.'

Words of condolence died on Lesley's lips. This wasn't the moment for encouragement. Fran had retreated into a mood of dejection and one false word now could either bring a sarcastic retort or cause her to clam up altogether. But by the time they walked to the gate together she was chatting again, albeit with some reserve. Lesley's promise to move in as soon as possible had raised her spirits again.

'When will you break it to Neil?' she asked.

'Tonight, I hope.' Lesley wasn't looking forward to this, for he too could be unpredictable. He might take her news with indifference or he could flare up with annoyance. It depended what kind of a day he had had.

She looked out across the bay and saw a full-rigged yacht skimming the waves like a fluttering bird, and drew Fran's attention to it. 'Isn't that *Seawife*?'

Fran squinted into the sun.

'No, it isn't, but it looks like her, doesn't it? It won't be long before *Seawife* is out there. What a lovely thought—a whole summer's sailing to look forward to! Lesley, you came to Trevaise just at the right time.'

Yes—but it all had to end in September, thought Lesley with a pang. And what had happened to her ambition to become a surgeon? Vanquished before the onslaught of a tall man with blue eyes and corn-gold hair! That didn't say much for her determination to succeed. But success comes in many forms, she argued with herself as she walked on down the hill.

CHAPTER SIX

LESLEY had the opportunity to speak to Neil on the subject of her move that same evening. They were on their own for dinner, Mrs Hatchet having gone off to a Churchwomen's meeting.

Neil seemed even more preoccupied than he had been that morning. He looked tired. His lids were heavy and once or twice Lesley saw him stifling a yawn. She knew he didn't spare himself on his operating days, and that afternoon he had gone straight from the hospital to one of the branch surgeries and then on to visit Mrs Fiske at High Moors. He made no move to open the yachting magazine at the side of his plate, and he didn't even look up when Lesley began to clear the table.

Mrs Hatchet had not left much washing up, she had dealt with the saucepans and baking tins before dishing up the meal. All Lesley found to do was the china and cutlery. She was putting away the last dish when Neil appeared.

'I've come to say I'm sorry I've been such poor company this evening. I'm bushed—' he stopped and looked round. 'You've done the washing-up! I wouldn't be in your shoes when Mrs H gets back—there'll be a battle royal over this!'

Lesley didn't enlighten him, but she had already had the battle royal—and won. Mrs Hatchet conceding a grudging defeat in the face of her persistence. Now she said, 'There's still some coffee left. Would you like to finish it up?'

'No—I need something stronger. As a matter of fact I came along to ask you to join me in my study. It's more cheerful, there's a fire.'

Though Lesley had never been in Neil's study she had looked in when passing if the door was open. From outside it looked a dull and bookish room, but now, inside and comfortably seated by an open fire, she realised she had been wrong. It was a cheerful room, its one large window overlooked the side of the garden and beyond she could see the rise of the moorland. The sun had just gone down behind the hills leaving in its wake a flaming path of orange and purple setting the whole of the western sky on fire. She guessed correctly that this was another room Neil's stepmother had not been allowed to make over, too much of its furniture was of his grandmother's period, perhaps earlier. There was an oil painting of a handsome young woman in Edwardian dress hanging over thc mantelpiece. Her hair was raven black and her eyes as brilliant as her grandson's. Except for the colour of her hair the likeness between the two was marked.

Neil stood by the drinks trolley and asked what she would have. She asked for a brandy and he gave her a drink the colour of liquid gold. He took a large gulp of his own, allowed it to rest in his mouth for a few seconds, then swallowed. 'Lord, how I needed that!' he said. Holding his glass up against the light, he squinted through it. 'What a colour! Like the essence of a flame to fire the flagging spirits.' He grinned. 'How's that for alliteration—after a day like today too!' He stared at his glass again.

'Do you know, my great-great-great grandfather was hanged for smuggling brandy like this into Trevaise. Not just once—he made quite a habit of it. Hanging him was the only way they could stop him.'

She stared at him. 'You're having me on!'

'I'm not—*she* told me.' He raised his glass in salute to his grandmother. 'She was proud of her notorious ancestor-in-law. She said he was the only Rodway who worked for his living, that the rest of the bunch only played at work.'

'She couldn't have said that about you,' said Lesley sincerely.

If he was surprised at her answer, he didn't show it. He was thoughtful for a moment or two. 'Actually when I told her I wanted to study medicine—guess what she said?' He didn't wait for an answer, but went on, 'She told me there was an old saying that—"shoemakers' children go barefoot and doctors' wives die young—" and not to forget it. I haven't.'

'But you haven't got a wife,' Lesley couldn't resist saying.

His lips twisted into a mocking smile. 'The Rodways take a long time to get to the married state, but they reach it in the end,' he said, putting a faint stress on the last word. She couldn't hold his gaze and looked away.

He finished his brandy, put down the empty glass and said, 'I really wanted to talk about Mrs Hatchet. I've been thinking over what you said about her and I think it would be a good idea if we got her to the hospital for a check-up. I would like Dr Hanson, the heart specialist, to see her, but unfortunately she knows him—he's visited here several times. She'd run a mile if I suggested it—not that she's got anything against Hanson, she likes him, but she'd fight like hell against any suggestion of anything wrong with her heart—and I'm not so sure I wouldn't agree with her. However, we've just appointed a bright young general physician to the hospital, and he'd give her the once-over for me. The question is —how to get her there.'

'She'd go if you told her to.'

He raised his eyebrows in a quizzical look. 'You overestimate my powers. In some ways I'm still a small boy in short trousers who used to visit here as far as she's concerned. No, I think she'd take more notice of you.'

Lesley was startled by this suggestion. 'Me? I don't think she's got a very good impression of me.'

'There you're wrong. She looked you up in the medical directory and was suitably impressed by your qualifications. Anyway, she likes you,' Neil added.

Lesley exploded. 'I don't believe it! Why, it's partly her attitude that decided me to move—' She stopped, but too late. She hadn't meant to break the news in this fashion. Neil's brows contracted into a frown.

'Did you say *move*?' His voice was ominous.

She placed her unfinished drink on the coffee table and reached for her handkerchief. Suddenly the palms of her hands were moist.

'I'm sorry, I didn't mean to blurt it out like that,' she said anxiously. 'I only decided today after talking to Fran. She wants me to move in to Cliff Cottage. It's not that I'm ungrateful for your hospitality,' she added hastily, seeing his face darken. 'You've all been very kind to me. But—but I have valid reasons for wanting to move—'

'You mean apart from Mrs Hatchet,' he said sarcastically.

Her cheeks reddened. This was going to be worse than she had expected. 'It would be more convenient for me to live nearer the surgery, especially as I haven't got a car. I'd be nearer most of the patients, so I could take my turn at being on call. As it is, I feel I'm not pulling my weight—'

He glowered at her. 'Don't talk such nonsense! You pull your weight and you know it. As for being on call—what about an emergency or an accident, for instance? How long would it take you to hoof it to the scene? You'll have to think up a better excuse than that!'

She should have known she couldn't hoodwink a man like Neil, but she couldn't allow him to suspect her real motive for wanting to leave Carn House. With some little effort she managed to answer in a cool manner, 'Do I have to make excuses for my actions?'

'I would appreciate the truth.' His voice was scathing.

'I've told you, it would be more convenient for me to live with Chris and Fran—and that's all I intend to say on the subject. I'm sorry if you've taken it as a personal affront—it wasn't meant that way.'

He didn't answer, just stared at her—studying the set of her chin, the defiance in her eyes. After a moment or two his lips began to twitch. 'I didn't know dark eyes could blaze, but yours do—they go black when you're angry. Don't glare at me like that—I'm sorry. Of course I've got no right to dictate where you should live. I'd overlooked the fact that you must miss London and all it has to offer. Fran will be more company for you than either Mrs H or myself, but of course Jan's going to miss you. It's for her sake I'd like you to stay.'

Lesley felt she could have done without the last remark. He wasn't personally worried about her going, then. His next words added further salt to her wounds.

'I thought you were such a self-contained sort of person, you could get along without company. Not like your predecessor, Dr Price. She tried living here, but not for long. She wanted a place of her own, but then she had a boy-friend to entertain. That isn't so in your case, is it?' His expression was wholly innocent, but there was a gleam in his eyes she didn't trust.

'That is entirely my own business,' she said coldly.

'I see.' He looked amused, then as if he had changed the subject he said quite diffidently, 'You know I called on Mrs Fiske today. She said her nephew is in New York, promoting an exhibition of some of his work. I gather it was a sudden decision, but perhaps you already knew about it?'

'And why should I?'

Again that look of innocence that didn't quite mask the speculation in his eyes.

'I got the impression that you two had—shall I say—hit it off. It had occurred to me he might be one of the reasons for you leaving here. You must have sensed that Colin Bucknall and I don't exactly like each other. Perhaps you thought it might be embarrassing for us all if he were to call on you here. That you'd have more freedom at Cliff Cottage.'

'And perhaps you've allowed your imagination to run away with you,' she retorted angrily. She rose to her feet so hastily she nearly sent the little table flying. 'If you'll excuse me, I have some chores to do before bedtime—'

'But you haven't finished your drink.'

'I've had quite enough, thank you.'

He followed her to the door. 'You mean you've had quite enough of me—and I don't blame you.' His voice was conciliatory, and his eyes—but she couldn't trust herself to look into his eyes.

'Please stay, Lesley, stay long enough to hear me out, anyway. I'm in a foul mood, and I have no excuse, though I have had a hell of a day. I had a lad to operate on who'd been in a motorbike accident. I had to take off one leg and I'm not too hopeful for the other. He's only eighteen, for God's sake! How the devil are we going to stop this carnage on the roads?' He stopped and breathed deeply as if to calm himself. He went on more quietly, 'What was it I said to you that first week? That you mustn't let yourself become personally involved with your patients in case it impaired your judgment. I'm a fine one to talk—I get involved all the time. Damn it—I care too much!' He looked down at her wistfully.

'I apologise for taking my feelings out on you—it wasn't anything you said, really, it was just that you were here.' The corners of his mouth turned up in a wry way. 'I won't do it again—but then I won't have the chance, will I? But we'll still see each other at the surgery, it's not a question of goodbye.'

'No,' said Lesley so calmly that he had no inkling of the turmoil inside her. Neil's rare mood of tenderness had disarmed her to the point that she began to regret her decision to move, but she still had enough sense to know she'd be doing the wisest thing. What she realised now was that Neil Rodway was becoming the most important factor in her life. Running away from him wouldn't change that, but it lessened the likelihood of his finding out.

When next morning Mrs Hatchet said in a subdued voice, 'I'm sorry to hear you're leaving us, Dr Colman. I hope it's not because of anything I've done or said. I know I'm a plain-spoken sort of person, but that's the way I am—I don't mean any harm. If I've offended you somehow, I'm sorry—' Lesley knew that Neil had already broken the news to her, perhaps last night when she returned from her meeting. Oh dear, she thought, why couldn't she just be allowed to leave quietly without having to smooth ruffled feelings—first Neil's, now Mrs

Hatchet's, and there was still Jan to come.

Earnestly she said, 'My move has nothing whatever to do with you, Mrs Hatchet. It's just that it would be more convenient for me to be nearer the surgery. And I'm very grateful for the way you've looked after me. Honestly, I haven't lived so well for years!'

'You won't go hungry at Mrs Watling's,' the housekeeper retorted dryly, but she looked mollified. 'And I want to thank you too, for being so tidy and keeping your room nice and clean. You've been no trouble to look after at all,' which confirmed Lesley's opinion that there was nothing so perverse as human nature.

On Sunday Neil was driving to St Ives to fetch Jan home, so Lesley decided that was an opportune time to make the switch, not hiding from herself the fact that she wanted to be out of Carn House before Jan returned. She felt she couldn't face another scene.

It was Chris who came to fetch her during the morning, when Mrs Hatchet was at church. 'I feel like some kind of a sneak-thief,' said Lesley as she closed the front door behind her. 'Creeping out when everyone is away, just as if I had a guilty conscience,' which wasn't inapt.

But Chris took a more commonsense point of view. 'Great Scott, you're not going to another planet, or even another town—you'll only be half a mile down the road! And you'll be good for Fran,' he added fervently. 'She needs somebody like you, cool-headed and reliable— (If you only knew, thought Lesley) she's very volatile, up in the clouds one minute, down in the depths the next. You'll have to make allowances for her.' His monkey eyes looked at her with great sadness.

Lesley was made to feel so much at home at Cliff Cottage that in a very few days it seemed that her life had always been like this. There were no hard and fast rules, no set times for meals, let alone anything else, but for all her easygoing routine Fran was a competent housewife. She was well prepared, her deep-freeze was always well stocked, and with her latest acquisition, a micro-wave oven, it was only a question of minutes before something appetising appeared on the table.

It didn't take Lesley very long to discover that Fran had one overriding fear, and that was for unexpected guests to arrive and find nothing to eat. It was this that accounted for the pies and cakes and flans she was always cooking for the deep-freeze. She confided in Lesley once that she had a recurring dream which had troubled her for years. In this dream she was surrounded by hungry guests and she had nothing to offer them. The dream took a variety of forms, but the theme was always the same: in their time of need she let her guests down.

'It's just one of those anxiety dreams caused by some deep inner frustration,' Lesley tried to explain.

'I know all about frustration,' Fran answered with a brittle laugh. She didn't enlarge on this, but Lesley understood.

Jan came to see Lesley with red-rimmed, reproachful eyes. To make things worse she had brought a gift from St Ives, a tiny statuette in the form of a little green elf. 'It's a Cornish Pisky,' she said listlessly. 'It's supposed to bring you good luck and a long life. I bought one for myself too, but it hasn't brought me any luck and I don't care about living long. I hope yours works better.'

Lesley went down on her knees and placed her hands on the girl's shoulders. 'Jan dear, I've only moved fifteen minutes' walk away—you'll get here in no time on your bike, and you know you'll always be welcome. I don't have to remind you how fond Fran is of you.'

Jan looked at Lesley from under her wet lashes. Her eyes, so like her brother's they made Lesley's heart lurch, were full of appeal.

'When I come will you help me with my homework?'

Lesley hugged her, her own tears not far away. 'I'll help you with anything, pet—your biology and chemistry and maths and French. Anything but history—I'm a dud at that!'

Jan smiled through her tears. 'And if you like, in exchange I'll teach you to sail,' she suggested.

Lesley looked thoughtfully past Jan's head. 'Y-yes,' she said slowly. 'That might be quite an idea.'

Another advantage Lesley had not reckoned on when moving to Cliff House was the use of Fran's car. Because of the fall of the land there was no garage at the cottage, but the Watlings rented a barn from a farmer lower down the hill and garaged both cars there. Now Fran often gave Lesley a lift when it was her turn to make house calls, and Lesley was hoping in time to be ferried backwards and forwards to the branch surgeries so that she could take her turn there as well.

To the surprise of them all Neil started popping in unexpectedly those evenings he had been working on his boat; this was usually between half-past ten and eleven at night. It was just a short visit, just time enough for a drink, and the conversation always veered around to *Seawife*. He now talked freely about his boat in front of Lesley, since Jan had let out that she already knew. As Fran had suspected, he had been waiting until the boat was launched before showing her off—but the next best thing was talking about her. Fran and Chris teased Lesley about his visits—or rather, they had an effective way of getting *at* her about them.

Fran would say something like, 'Strange the way Neil

keeps dropping in. Do you think it's my shortbread biscuits? He seems to enjoy them.' And Chris usually retorted, 'It's nothing to do with your biscuits, it's my malt whisky,' then they would both look at Lesley with guileless eyes. 'What do you think the attraction is, Lesley—the biscuits or the whisky?'

Lesley soon took their measure. 'It's my charms, of course,' she said once, and from then on the teasing stopped. But in the privacy of her room she couldn't help giving in to wishful thinking. Just supposing she was the reason for Neil's visits? Was it too hard to believe? She hugged the possibility to herself. By leaving Carn House it had been brought home to her how much Neil meant to her. She missed his presence. His strong and at times overwhelming personality had dominated Carn House. She found she missed his tread on the stairs, the carefree whistling when he was in a happy mood, even the way he shouted in exasperation when something he wanted had been misplaced. She was not yet ready to admit that she was in love with him, but she was perilously near the brink. Could it be possible he missed her too—was that what brought him to the cottage?

No. Hers wasn't a personality that left its mark. She couldn't stand in the moonlight and twine her arms round a man's neck. And what had happened to *her*—that unknown girl? Had she slipped out of Neil's life, and if so was that why he sought other company? Was he just marking time until he had found somebody else to take the girl's place? It was a thought that stabbed Lesley continuously.

By this time old Bert Gooley no longer needed medical attention. For the time being the ulcer on his leg had healed, but Lesley still called in to see him if she was in the vicinity of his cottage. She would encourage him to tell her tales about 'that young imp, Master Neil' and the tricks he got up to as a lad. From the old man she built up a picture of a different Neil, a devil-may-care young boy with a love of adventure, and wondered sometimes if he didn't have something in common with his smuggler ancestor. One day after seeing Bert she went on to call on a Mrs Bourne who lived in a council house nearby. Her son had left a message to say his mother was having trouble with her knee, and would one of the doctors call, but not to come especially as it wasn't urgent.

When Neil told Lesley he had added, 'I know Mrs Bourne. She's the sort who wouldn't complain if she had one foot in the grave and the other on a banana skin. Go as soon as you can, it could be graver than she's making out.'

The Woodside Estate where Mrs Bourne lived had been developed between the wars, and was large by Trevaise standards, consisting of fifty houses. They were all semi-detached and substantially built of pebbledash walls and slate roofs. Compared with the whitewashed cottages of the harbour area they appeared strictly utilitarian, but the gardens made up in colour and imagination for what the houses lacked. Mrs Bourne's was one of the exceptions. Here there was an old car without wheels jacked up in her sideway, and a motorbike in pieces on what could have been a lawn. As she walked up to the front door Lesley had to avoid stepping on loose nuts and bolts or globules of oil.

She knocked and waited. Presently she heard the sounds of a slow and difficult passage of someone coming along the hall. The woman who opened the door to her was in her late fifties, broad-faced and broad-hipped, her skirt pulled up by a tight apron was short enough to reveal one grossly swollen knee.

Lesley could smell baking. 'I hope I haven't called at an awkward moment,' she began. 'I'm Dr Colman, Dr Rodway's new assistant.'

Mrs Bourne had large patient eyes.

'Come in, Doctor, come in,' she said, opening the door wider. 'I'm just warming up some pasties for supper, but they'll keep. In here, please.' She opened a door immediately on her left. The best room, thought Lesley, kept for Sundays and parties. It was uncomfortably tidy, and a vase of plastic daffodils stood dead centre on the mantelpiece.

'Be seated, Doctor,' invited Mrs Bourne, plumping up a cushion on a chintz-covered armchair.

'No. You be seated, Mrs Bourne, I want to examine that knee.'

Both knees were badly misshapen with arthritis, but the right one was more inflamed and tender to the touch. Lesley satisfied herself there was no fluid present, though there was swelling and pain and it felt hot beneath her hand.

'How long have you had this trouble?' she asked.

'Oh, I've had pains in my legs for years, Doctor. Well, you expect to when you're over fifty, don't you? Last summer, during the hot spell, my knee played up something terrible. It burned and ached so I could only get comfort by putting a wet compress on it. Then it wasn't so bad during the winter, so I thought it had cleared up on its own. I mean, I know I've got arthritis, I've had it for years, but I didn't like to complain about that —there's some far worse. Look at poor Mrs Trevor down the road, she—'

'I'm more concerned about you at present, Mrs Bourne. How long has your knee been swollen like this?'

'It came up again two weeks ago when we had those

few warm days. It's the heat that does it, Doctor. I can't bear to sit by a fire, and I can't bear the weight of bedclothes on my knee either. I usually stick my leg out of the side of the bed.'

Lesley rose to her feet. 'You'll have to see an orthopaedic surgeon about this, but first he'll require X-rays to see the extent of the damage. I'll make an appointment for you at the hospital.'

A look of alarm crossed the woman's face. 'I won't have to have an operation, will I? I mean, there's nothing seriously wrong, it's only arthritis—'

'It's more than that, Mrs Bourne. I think the arthritis has affected your knee-cap and now that is diseased. Walking must be agony for you?'

'It is rather, but standing still is even worse, like when I'm ironing, or washing up, or cooking.'

'And there's nobody to help you?'

The large eyes turned wistful. 'Not since my daughter married and moved to Falmouth. My husband's good when he's at home, but he's away so much—he's a cook on an oil-tanker. There's my boy Steve, but he has his own work to do.'

'And what's that?' asked Lesley, thinking of the dismembered vehicles in the front garden.

'He's self-employed at the moment,' said Mrs Bourne proudly. 'He buys up old cars and bikes and does them up and sells them again. He only just started last winter when he was made redundant, so he's not making much money at it yet, but he will—he will,' she added confidently.

When Lesley was ready to go Mrs Bourne struggled up in order to see her out, but was gently pushed back. 'No, you stay there. Rest is all-important, Mrs Bourne, and try to do your ironing sitting down in future. Not so much standing about, eh? By the way, have you got a fridge? Good. Then wrap some ice-cubes in a tea-towel or bandage or anything suitable and tie it round your knee. It will relieve the pain and reduce the swelling. Try that just before you go to bed and I'll send Nurse round with some pain-killing tablets. They will help you to sleep better.'

Neil had just returned from visiting a branch surgery as Lesley got back from her rounds. Both were free for a short while and Lesley was able to tell him about Mrs Bourne.

'I think the patella is damaged due to a chronic arthritis. At the moment it's in an acute stage—extremely painful. I've seen cases like it before at St Bede's—' she stopped, seeing the way he smiled, then the blood rushed to her face as she remembered with embarrassment that though she could count in dozens the cases of diseased patellas she had seen during her hospital training—in all probability he had not only seen but operated on many times that number.

Wretchedly she said, 'I keep forgetting about your other hat.'

He laughed goodhumouredly. 'Sometimes I wish I could! But about Mrs Bourne—I'll go up and have a look at her myself this evening, and if I confirm your findings I'll see she gets an X-ray some time next week.'

'Won't that mean jumping the queue?'

'And don't you think Mrs Bourne deserves a little priority after putting up with pain like that all these months?'

He was using the same tone of voice as he had when he called her a prig. Why is it, she asked herself in despair, I always say the wrong thing at the wrong time? Why can't I ever say the right thing at the right time!

It was now mid-May. Swallows were skimming over the meadows and all day long a persistent cuckoo called from a nearby spinney, and in the woods bluebells made a close-set sweet-smelling carpet. It was a time for rejoicing, and in spite of her unfulfilled longings Lesley found her pulses quicken by the challenge of spring.

The three medicos took it in turns to have an afternoon a week off and on Lesley's free afternoons Fran would often suggest a drive out to one of the local beauty spots. In this way Lesley was not only learning more about Cornwall, she was increasingly falling under its spell. One such afternoon Fran said she had thought of something different. They'd go to the next cove with a picnic tea.

'Why not here, in Trevaise?' queried Lesley. 'You wouldn't have to use the car then.'

'Because there's something very special about Pencade. I'll tell you on the way.'

Pencade, Fran went on to relate, was a deserted village about three miles farther west. Fifty years ago it had been a flourishing little fishing community, not as large as Trevaise, but prosperous in a limited fashion. As it was surrounded on three sides by steep cliffs the only approach to it was by sea or the track that zigzagged down the cliff face, and because of its isolation Pencade had the name of being unfriendly and stand-offish. Then one dreadful night of storm and high winds the sea rose like a tidal wave and washed away nearly the whole of the village. A few inhabitants survived, among them a beautiful young girl, but her mother and father, her brothers, and girlhood sweetheart were all drowned. When rescuers finally came she refused to leave with the other survivors. 'This is my home, and I'm staying!' she said stubbornly—and she did, and she still does,' Fran finished with a dramatic fall of her voice.

'She doesn't! How old would that make her, for goodness' sake?'

'In her late sixties, early seventies—I'm not sure, she looks ageless. It's amazing how she's survived all these years. Chris says she's pickled in dirt.'

'And I presume you're taking me to see this remarkable old woman.'

Fran grinned. 'I thought it would make a change from all the pretty sights I've been showing you lately! No cream teas this afternoon—just sandwiches on the beach.'

They left the car at the entrance to the cove, then walked along the rising cliff path until they came to the track which led to the deserted village. A deserted village sounded romantic, but it wasn't—all that remained of one-time homes was mounds of broken granite. One cottage had been made habitable after a fashion, patched up with driftwood. Lesley wouldn't have stabled a horse in it. She was amazed when an incredibly dirty and ugly old woman came out—how could it possibly be anyone's home! She stared in disbelief at the wizened old crone. Could she ever have been 'a beautiful young girl'? It was difficult even to see her colouring under the grime of years. Her hair looked like a mass of soap pads wadded together, but her eyes were as bright and as black as jet. She grinned at them, revealing three yellow teeth, and when she spoke her voice creaked with disuse.

'Welcome to my village, ladies,' she chortled. 'Welcome to Pencade. Have you come to be shown round?'

Fran whispered, 'She'll expect a tip.'

Surprisingly the old lady was as sure-footed as a goat

as she led them in a scramble over the rocks. Her name was Nellie Briggs. Lesley noticed that Fran addressed her politely as Miss Briggs. There wasn't much left of the village to see, and what there was Lesley found rather sad—like the iron spars of the vanished jetty which stuck out of the water like broken claws. Afterwards both girls gave the old woman a substantial tip and saw her eyes gleam, but they gleamed even more brightly over the tea and sugar Fran had thought to bring her.

'Would you like to stay and have tea with me, ladies? I haven't any milk, but then we never did have fresh milk in Pencade,' she tittered.

They made their excuses and left, and as they walked away Lesley said, 'My heart turned over when she invited us to tea. For one awful moment I thought you were going to accept. What does she use for water?'

'There's a fresh-water spring that bubbles out of the cliff.'

'It's a pity she doesn't use it to wash in, then,' said Lesley crossly. 'I can't understand the Public Health people. Why haven't they taken her into care?'

'Perhaps they realise that would be the surest way of killing her,' retorted Fran. 'My goodness, Lesley, you can be stuffy at times! Don't you see anything at all romantic about old Nellie Briggs?'

'Romantic? No, I don't! She's a pathetic old woman who needs a bath more than anything else, one with lashings of disinfectant in it. However did she come to fall through the welfare net, I wonder—and don't ask me to believe she was ever young and beautiful!'

'Then ask Bert Gooley. He was in love with her once!'

Fran marched on, indignation flaming her thin cheeks. The tide had fallen and they were walking back to the car along the beach. Lesley ran to catch her up.

'You're like Chris,' Fran said brokenly. 'You can't see romance in anything but sterile operating theatres or antiseptic surgeries. Oh, Lesley, stop being a doctor and start being a woman, or you'll end up like me—all shrivelled up and empty inside.'

Lesley slipped her arm through Fran's. The sun was warm on their backs. Quick little brown birds darted about the tideline in quest of food, colonies of kittiwakes fought for nesting places on the cliff ledges, and the sea, shimmering like green shot silk, lapped gently on the wet sand. 'I can see romance in all this beauty around us,' she said. 'But I can't see anything romantic about your deserted village, except possibly its name. Don't you think poor old Nellie Briggs would be better off in care?'

'How do you think she's survived all these years?' said Fran truculently. 'She's tough and independent. She'd die if you took her away from her home.'

'She'd die if you and others like you stopped giving her food and money. What would happen to her if she were to fall ill—or have a fall and break a leg or something? Have you thought of that?'

Fran sighed impatiently. 'The ever-practical Lesley, with an answer for everything! Oh, I'm sorry, I didn't mean to snap at you like that. Of course you're right, but don't you see, she's become a legend, and I don't want to see that legend die. I'm Cornish too, you know, I share her fierce pride in our homeland—I would fight to keep my identity too if I were her.'

They said no more about old Nellie until they were sitting with their backs to the cliffs, a flask of tea and sandwiches between them, then Fran brought up the subject again. She had been staring broodingly at the receding waves when suddenly she remarked, 'I nearly called on her for help, once.'

Caught unawares, Lesley said, 'Who?'

'Nellie Briggs. People around here say she's a witch, and of course she plays on it. She collects herbs from the cliff-top and boils them down into potions, cures for all kinds of things. Rheumatism, heart trouble, boils, poor eyesight, deafness—and even mundane things like unrequited love and childlessness.'

Lesley caught her breath. 'Fran, you can't mean—? You wouldn't go to that simple-minded old woman for that!'

Fran answered with a certain amount of bravado. 'When anyone has been married for ten years and is beginning to get desperate—yes, they would try witch-craft.'

With an effort Lesley kept calm. 'You know there's medical help for women like you—and I don't only mean the fertility pill. But you'd rather try witchcraft. I don't understand you.'

'And what is this medical help, as you call it, but a modern form of witchcraft!'

Lesley saw there was no point in arguing with Fran in her present frame of mind. 'Please, Fran, don't let's quarrel,' she begged. 'But promise me you won't go to Nellie Briggs for any reason. If you want help come to me or Neil—or better still, Chris. You see, apart from anything else, we really care.'

No other words could have touched Fran so effect-ively. Her rancour and bitterness fell away. With a half sob she said:

'Bear with me, Lesley—bear with me until this mood has passed.' She smiled faintly. 'But not to worry, I won't submit to old Nell's witchcraft any more than I would submit to yours. Do you know what I tell myself sometimes?' Her voice had become self-mocking. 'That some time a girl will walk into the surgery and tell you or one of the others that she's pregnant and unable to keep the baby and wanted to find someone suitable to adopt it. And I shall be waiting. There, what's more romantic than that?'

Romantic, yes—also strangely prophetic, as Lesley was to find out to her cost in the very near future.

CHAPTER SEVEN

It was eight-thirty and Lesley was walking leisurely home. She had just finished the evening surgery and was in no hurry to get indoors, the evening was too perfect to waste.

After two days of continuous rain the sun had re-appeared that morning and was still shining, and Lesley was beginning to regret the new raincoat she had bought on her last payday. Fran had been the deciding factor. 'In Cornwall the most essential part of one's wardrobe is a good raincoat, and your old one, if you don't mind me saying so, has had it!' she said, and there was no arguing with that.

Neither did Chris and Fran want to stay indoors on such an evening; Lesley found them on the patio with drinks in their hands. With a bank of brilliant red rhododendrons behind them and the limpid sea below it was easy to imagine them somewhere on the Riviera.

'Supper will be ready in half an hour, join us in an aperitif first,' said Fran lazily. She patted the empty chair beside her.

Lesley seated herself with a sigh of justification. She felt she deserved this—it had been a hard day, but a good one, with few problems. Best of all had been the phone call from the District Hospital to say they were booking Mrs Bourne for an X-ray examination at the earliest possible moment.

Chris went in to get her a drink but reappeared almost

at once. 'Call for you, Lesley. It's your old friend from St Bede's—James Stimpson.'

It must be the news of Karen Lesley had been waiting for for the past week. She hurried in to the phone.

James sounded jubilant. 'Wotcha, Les ole girl—I'm back in the happy father stakes. Twins—both boys—and all three doing well!'

'*Twins!* Have you known all along—?'

'Only Karen and myself, and we let little Amy in on it, of course.'

'You rotter, you might have told me too!'

'You know what they say, Les—many a slip 'twixt the cup and the lip. *Now* you're the first to know.'

Lesley's eyes grew sentimentally moist.

'Oh, James, I'm so delighted! Do give Karen my love and tell her I think she's a very clever woman. You're sure she's okay?'

'Blooming—I wish you could see for yourself. She has babies like shelling peas—nothing to it, she says. Now all she wants is to come home and share them with Amy. Any chance of you paying us a visit soon, Lesley? We're both longing to see you again.'

Lesley thought quickly. 'I was planning to come up early next month to see Aunt Celia. She'll be seventy on June the fourth and I'd like to be with her on her birthday—'

'That would work out fine,' James interrupted eagerly. 'Karen will be up and about by then. You'll stay with us, of course?'

'I'll discuss that with Karen later,' Lesley just managed to say before the pips sounded. James was calling from a callbox at the hospital. Thoughtfully she replaced the receiver. Her first reaction had been to dash into the garden with the good news, but now she hesitated. How would Fran take it? Might she not think—'Here's a woman with one child already, now she has another two babies, and I can't have one'. The slightest thing sent her into a fit of melancholy. Still undecided, Lesley walked slowly to the door—and suddenly heard the deep rich tone of the voice that had the power to make her heart lurch. Neil had called, and Karen and her baby sons went right out of her mind.

He was sitting astride one of the chairs, his long legs stretched out in front of him. He looked up with a goodhumoured smile, his eyes strikingly intense. 'Hi, Lesley,' he said. 'This includes you too. What are you doing on June the fourth?'

She stared. Was he a thought-reader? Could he possibly know about her aunt's birthday? He didn't wait for her answer.

'It's my birthday and I'm giving a small party at the Yacht Club—I'm launching *Seawife* that afternoon too, so it will be a double celebration. You'll be there?'

'Of course she will,' put in Chris. 'Nothing will keep her away, will it, Lesley? The gang must keep together on these occasions!'

Lesley had a brief tussle with her conscience and lost. She could go down to Sussex and see Aunt Celia the following weekend, in her present state of health the poor dear would know nothing about her birthday or even what a birthday meant—she might not know Lesley, even. It was so easy to tell herself that and then to say aloud, 'Yes, I'd love to come.'

Chris said, 'You're late getting your old tub launched this year, aren't you?'

'They kept me waiting ages for that new mast I wanted, and then I've been making some alterations in the saloon, as you shall see on June the fourth. Not to worry, a fine summer has been predicted—I'll be able to make up for lost time.' Neil wouldn't stay any longer, not even for a drink. He wanted to get on to the Club to book a room for the party.

When he had gone Fran asked the question Lesley had been dreading: 'Any news from your friends in London?'

Trying not to show delight, Lesley told them about the twins' arrival in as few words as possible, even so she saw Fran freeze. Then with an effort she assumed a brittle smile. 'How lucky for them,' she said crisply. Tight-lipped, she gathered up the used glasses and went into the house. Lesley made to follow her, but Chris held her back. 'Let her go,' he said quietly.

'I was only going to help with the supper.'

'I don't think she wants any help. For the moment she'd rather be alone.' Chris looked with his sad monkey eyes towards the house. 'Poor Fran, she'll get over it—she's had years of practice.'

The following morning, just as Lesley took her place at her desk, Miss Pearson phoned through to her.

'Dr Colman, a personal call for you—long-distance.'

Instantly Lesley thought of Karen and the twins—was anything wrong? But it wasn't James on the phone, it was a woman speaking in a sepulchral voice that Lesley didn't recognise. It was the Matron of the Belvedere, using the tones she kept for bad news.

'Dr Colman, I'm very sorry to have to tell you that your aunt passed away during the night. She didn't suffer at all, she died quite peacefully in her sleep. I now await your instructions. You will be coming to the Nursing Home?'

Was there just a touch of reproach in those last words? In her shattered state Lesley felt sensitive enough to believe anything—especially against herself. The inner recriminations began as soon as she had replaced the phone.

Why hadn't she been to see Aunt Celia before this? —sending a weekly postcard had been an easy way to salve her conscience. Even her plan to visit her aunt on her birthday had been quickly shelved when a more attractive invitation had come her way. It hurt more to realise that others considered her the perfect niece. The news that she contributed to her aunt's keep was known to Neil and Chris and Fran—she suspected through James. What would they think of her if she told them that easing her own conscience meant more to her than easing the last years of her aunt's life? In her present state of mind she was ready to believe anything of herself. With hot dry eyes she went in to tell Chris.

He gave one look at her stricken face and came towards her to put a comforting arm round her shoulders.

'I'll phone Fran to fetch you,' he said at once. 'And I'll get Neil on the car radio, he's only just left for Pringle and Polhearne. There's no question of you working today, you'll want to get to London as soon as possible.'

Lesley had to pull herself together; there was a lot to do. Fran ran her into Roshaven to go to the bank, and it was Fran who suggested tentatively that she bought something suitable to wear to the funeral and helped her choose a plain grey silk blouse. But it was Neil who was her chief mainstay. He phoned the station to get the time of her train; he booked her a first-class seat, and insisted on driving her to Penzance himself.

'There's no need for you to rush back here,' he said as they approached the outskirts of the town. He didn't add 'after the funeral', but that was what he meant. 'I can easily arrange for a locum for a few days. I suppose you'll stay with James and Karen?'

At the mention of their names Lesley roused herself from her unquiet thoughts. She had yet to tell Neil their good news. 'I didn't like to mention it last night,' she explained now. 'Not in front of Fran. It didn't seem right to feel glad then, and it seems even worse to feel glad about it this morning.'

He placed a firm warm hand over hers. 'Grieve all you want, Lesley, don't bottle it up—but don't wallow either. You'll need all your strength to face the next few days.'

She couldn't look at him, she was too fearful of breaking down. Tears would have been a relief, but she didn't want to cry—not in front of Neil—she still took a silly pride in her façade of a woman of strength. But she was deeply grateful to him for his silent sympathy.

Her train was waiting in Penzance station. Neil found her seat and lifted her overnight case on to the rack. She had brought the minimum of luggage and if necessary could buy anything she wanted in London. She wouldn't have to look at every penny in future. She tried not to think that, it only added to her load of guilt, but the thought persisted.

'Thank you for all you've done for me,' she said as Neil stood with her outside her compartment. He took the hand she held out and pulled on it, gently drawing her nearer. She did not resist, neither did she consciously make a movement towards him, but somehow she was in his arms and his lips were seeking hers, and she submitted willingly to his gentle demands.

He lifted his head and stepped back to look at her with his incredible blue eyes ablaze with such ardour that she felt shaken. In spite of her grief and the oppression which seemed like a weight on her shoulders her reaction was one of unbounded joy, for she knew now that this man meant more to her than anyone else in the world. That, quite simply, she was in love.

He walked away without a word, and she watched him stride out of her sight before taking her seat. She stared unseeingly out of the window as the train pulled away. Why had he kissed her? To show his sympathy—his concern? No, it wasn't that kind of a kiss. She put her fingers up to her mouth, imagining she could still feel the pressure of his lips, and then unbidden came the thought of other women he had kissed—perhaps in the same manner. Her hopes died a little. She was not unique, she was just one of many.

The train throbbed into Paddington, and there was James faithfully waiting. Probably Neil had phoned him about her coming to London, and also to congratulate him. He gave her a swift hug. 'Come along, I'm getting you home as quickly as possible. You look as if you haven't slept for days, and I don't suppose you had anything to eat on the train either.' He ushered her through the crowds and out into the station forecourt.

His car was parked some distance away. It was no problem finding it; it was getting out of the stream of traffic in the streets around the station that took time. It wasn't until they were out of the City precincts and heading east towards Wanstead that James brought up the subject of Aunt Celia.

Lesley told him in a few broken sentences; she had not much news other than what Matron had given her over the phone. She would know more when she visited the nursing home; then she asked after Karen and also wanted to know who was looking after Amy.

'Our daily, Mrs Geary—then I take over at night. Neighbours have been very helpful too. Amy is expecting you to put her to bed tonight. I hope you feel up to it.'

'It will help take my mind off things,' said Lesley, smiling for the first time that day. She remembered other times when she had given Amy her bedtime bath and then had read to her afterwards. That little bundle of charm and energy would dispel any gloom!

Early the following morning she travelled down to Sussex. She found a hotel near the Belvedere and booked in for three days, then walked the half-mile to the nursing home. The last time she had travelled this lane in early April the trees had only just begun to green over, now in late May they were in full leaf and nesting birds fluttered restlessly among their branches. Matron was expecting her and had coffee waiting in her office. In spite of her annoying little mannerisms and a professional brightness that sometimes jarred, she was a warmhearted woman who really cared about her patients. Aunt Celia's collection of private possessions, and it was pitifully small, was in a neat pile awaiting Lesley's instructions. 'I'll leave you alone to go through them,' Matron said tactfully as she withdrew.

Sorting through the documents, Lesley came across an old school photograph of herself and her school reports in their right order. Aunt Celia had treasured them all these years, all the time Lesley thought she hadn't cared. At last her tears came, she couldn't stop them—and afterwards, though she felt drained of emotion, the feeling of oppression had gone.

Matron judged the time nicely to make her reappearance. Composed but pale, Lesley sat at the window staring into the distance. Matron said in the gentle tones she reserved for grieving relatives, 'Would you like to see your aunt's room now? It's been made ready for the next occupant, but there are some pieces of furniture from your aunt's old home you may want to have.'

There was no point in seeing the room; Lesley would rather remember it as it was on her last visit, when she and Aunt Celia had achieved a kind of closeness they had never had before. As for the furniture, if it could be of use to someone else it might as well stay there, she told Matron.

James came down for the funeral. It was a wet cold day and the wind had veered round to the north-west. The service at the crematorium was short and simple, but Lesley found it very moving. The rain had stopped but the skies were still black as they drove back to London that afternoon. Suddenly a shaft of sunlight broke through the clouds and there in the opposite sky appeared an unbroken rainbow. Lesley watched as it faded into an indistinct blur. 'Do you think that was a happy omen?' she said hopefully.

And James answered sincerely, 'I once read that a rainbow is a bridge to peace. For your aunt's sake it would be nice to believe that.'

Karen was home, released from hospital on condition that she went straight to bed, but she had stayed up to welcome Lesley. It was Amy who had gone to bed.

'With a diplomatic headache,' said Karen, pulling a face at her husband. 'She's a funny little scrap. You know how excited she was about the twins, she looked on them as a pair of live dolls we'd bought for her to play with? Well, today they disgraced themselves, they wouldn't stop bawling, and finally she came to me with a very plaintive look and said, 'Mummy, could we take them back now and have a Paddington Bear instead?' Actually she's beginning to feel just a slight dislocation of her nose.'

James grinned. 'I'll go up to her,' he said. 'I'll read her one of her favourite fairy tales.'

The night before Lesley was due to return to Trevaise, she and Karen had the chance to sit and talk on their own as James had returned to the hospital to attend a committee meeting. Amy was genuinely asleep this time, and with her out of the way, Karen had brought the twins down for a feed and a cuddle, and now, brimming with milk and limp with sleep, they lay one on each of the girls' laps.

Lesley ran the back of her finger softly against the satiny skin of the baby's cheek. She looked at the sweep of the well-defined eyebrows, the long upturned lashes, each perfectly formed fingernail, and felt the first awakening of a maternal hunger. It gave her a glimpse into Fran's hopeless longing. She looked up to see Karen watching her.

'Does he meet with your approval?' she asked laughingly. 'By the way, that's David you're holding —I've got Jonathan. We decided last night—after an argument, I don't mind admitting. James thinks my choice is awfully corny, but I like Biblical names. We're having the christening in September on our wedding anniversary,' she added. 'You'll have finished your job in Trevaise by then, won't you? We'd love you to be one of the godmothers.'

Such a sensation of despair went over Lesley at Karen's words that she found her hands tightening on the sleeping child. Leave Trevaise—she didn't want to think of that possibility, because that would mean leaving Neil. She said quickly, 'Of course I'll be godmother, whether I'm still in Cornwall or not. I'll make time for that important date!'

Karen looked relieved. 'You don't have to worry about staying in Cornwall, you know. James didn't intend to say anything until it's an absolute cert, but he's pretty sure you'll get the next vacancy at St Bede's, and there's a senior house surgeon's post coming up in late September. That should please you.'

But there was nothing that resembled pleasure in Lesley's expression. Karen stared.

'You *do* still want to return to St Bede's, don't you? You must feel very cut off from everything where you are. Though I must admit Cornwall agrees with you—you're radiant! You don't need make-up with that glorious colour, and I like your hair like that—thank goodness you've stopped chewing it. But why so sad, Lesley—?' She stopped herself with a sharp intake of breath. 'What a crass idiot I am! Of course, you're still upset about your aunt.'

That was part of Lesley's worry, but not the main part. She said wistfully, 'If only I'd shown her I loved her while she was still alive! Now it's too late.'

Gently Karen answered, 'I'm one of those simple souls who believes she knows that now.' She rose, baby Jonathan in the crook of her right arm, and holding out her free arm to Lesley. 'Balance me up,' she said. 'Give me David—it's time our sons and heirs were in their cots.'

'You can't manage both at once! You'll trip or drop one of them or something silly. I'll carry David up.'

But Karen was insistent. 'I've got to learn to do this unaided, I won't always have help, and in any case I've been practising. And weren't you going to ring Neil to tell him what time your train gets to Penzance tomorrow?'

Lesley waited until Karen was upstairs before going to the phone. Remembering how they had parted, she felt selfconscious at the thought of speaking to Neil before a third party. She needn't have worried; Neil wasn't in and neither was Jan. Mrs Hatchet answered the phone. Lesley didn't stay long talking, the housekeeper's deafness made conversation difficult. She hung up just as Karen returned.

'Get through all right?'

Lesley stood frowning. 'I hope so. Poor Mrs Hatchet, she'll have to do something about her hearing soon, it's getting worse, but I know she'd jump down my throat if I suggested a hearing aid.'

'Perhaps she just needs her ears syringing.' Karen walked across to the television and switched on the news. 'Now for twenty-five minutes of gloom,' she said wryly. 'Shall we have a drink to counteract it, and I've got the remains of a box of chocolates somewhere.'

James took Lesley to Paddington the next day, but he didn't stop to wave the train out as he had an outpatients' clinic to attend. He gave her a hasty peck on the cheek, handed over her case and some sandwiches Karen had made, and was off. The train was already in and Lesley went straight to her seat. It had been something of a treat to see old London again. The sight of the familiar red buses had given her a twinge of nostalgia, but now she was returning to Cornwall, and she felt she was going home.

She knew she was back in the West Country as soon as she stepped out of the train at Penzance. Again she had the sensation as of silk against her face as the soft wind blew off Mount's Bay. There was no sign of Neil, but she wasn't worried. It was a fine afternoon—he might have been delayed, and she didn't mind waiting. She walked out of the station and towards the harbour; she hadn't seen much of Penzance on her first visit, but now she had time 'to stand and stare'. It was rewarding. The harbour was a spectacular sight, the waters constantly astir with the passage of boats all with their following of keening, flocking gulls. The ferries left from here to sail to the Scilly Isles, a two-and-a-half-hour journey away. Lesley had promised herself a holiday there at the end of the season. To her left the small granite island of St Michael's Mount rose out of the wide curve of the bay, the castle on its summit clearly visible in the transparent atmosphere. It was the cleanness of the air that struck her afresh after the pollution of London. Could she possibly go back there to work after this? Would she have the choice?

She walked slowly back to the station. Neil still had not arrived, and now she began to wonder if he had received her message. She decided to give him another fifteen minutes and if he hadn't come by then to walk up to the town centre and enquire about a bus to Roshaven.

The minutes dragged past. With a sinking heart she realised he wasn't coming. It wasn't that she minded the long journey to Roshaven so much as disappointment at not seeing him here where they had last been together. That parting had been so fraught with emotion for her, had left her hoping it had had the same effect on him, so that his non-appearance was something of an anti-climax.

Reluctantly she made her way along the promenade, meaning to cross the road farther up to go towards the main part of the town, but she had only gone a few yards when she heard her name called. It couldn't be Neil; it wasn't his deep voice. She turned and watched a slight dark man coming towards her, wondering who it could be. Then she noticed he walked with a faint limp and realised it was Colin Bucknall. She hadn't recognised him, simply because she had forgotten what he looked like.

He caught her up, slightly out of breath. 'I couldn't trust my luck when I saw you, and I knew it must be you—you're the only tall blonde goddess I know in these parts.'

Lesley was too travel-weary and her mind in too much of a turmoil to react to shallow pleasantries. She smiled briefly, and when he asked where she had come from, she just said London, without giving any reasons.

'How are you getting back to Trevaise?' asked Colin. 'Is someone meeting you?'

'Someone was, but I don't think my message got through. I was about to enquire about a bus—'

He didn't attempt to disguise his delight at this piece of information. 'Good, now I can take you home. My car's just along here.' He steered her back towards the station yard, and she made no effort to resist—she would have been glad of a lift from anybody.

Colin began to apologise for not getting in touch before. He explained, 'I had this sudden call to New York, then I went on to San Francisco. I wanted to write to you, but thought it would be politic not to do so, considering the way Neil Rodway feels about me. I didn't think he'd take kindly to one of his guests receiving mail from me.'

She said stiffly, 'I'm no longer living at Carn House. I've moved in with the Watlings at Cliff Cottage.'

His dark eyes shone with a sudden malice. 'So the stiffnecked Dr Rodway got too much for you too in the end, did he?'

Lesley turned on him angrily. 'He did not! It's just that it's more convenient for me to be nearer the practice—' She couldn't trust herself to say anything more, but hurried on, wanting to get away from him as quickly as possible—but then she heard his faltering footsteps as he tried to catch her up and remorse got the better of her. 'I'm sorry,' she said. 'I'm too touchy, I can't help it. I'm tired, and—and my journey wasn't a happy one.'

He looked grave. 'I'm the one who should be apologising. Here's my car. You tuck down and sleep if you feel like it.'

Sleep was impossible; Colin wasn't a natural driver like Neil. Sometimes he was so over-cautious he was a menace to other drivers, and at other times he took risks that made her toes turn under. She gave up trying to compose herself and sat up and listened instead. He had a lot to relate about his exhibitions in the States. They had been so successful he had been asked to give others in the autumn.

'Have you thought any more about me painting you?' he asked her suddenly.

This took her by surprise. 'Why me? You must know scores of women!'

'I do, but it's you I want to paint.' He hesitated. 'There's something about you that reminds me of Rosemary—my wife.'

This was the first she knew that he was married. 'Your wife? I didn't realise—'

'Why should you—she's been dead several years.' There was such a note of finality about his voice that Lesley didn't pursue the subject.

At last they were on the outskirts of Trevaise. She looked with contented eyes on the woods and narrow lanes, the granite cottages and the large houses in their spacious grounds. And best of all, the view of the tiny harbour and the blue-green water of Trevaise Bay as they drew up outside Cliff Cottage.

Lesley felt she had to ask Colin to come in for a drink, but he declined. He explained that he had only returned from America the day before, had spent most of that day in Penzance renewing his stock of artist's materials and didn't like to leave his aunt alone any longer.

'But the trip to Penzance was worthwhile. It brought me you,' he said significantly.

She was impatient to get in to Fran, impatient with Colin's constant insinuations, but she thanked him politely for bringing her home and held out her hand.

He took it, turned it over and left a long slow kiss on her palm. She reddened, but he only grinned—then as he drove off she saw Neil striding down the hill towards her, his face black with rage. He drew level and glowered at her. 'Why didn't you let me know you were returning today? I would have come to Penzance for you as we arranged, but obviously you changed your mind!'

Seeing Colin with her, seeing his amorous leavetaking, he had jumped to the conclusion that their meeting had been prearranged. She was hurt that he could think her guilty of such duplicity. She had so looked forward to seeing him again—but not like this, with mistrust making his eyes glitter like blue ice.

She explained emphatically, 'I *did* phone. I spoke to Mrs Hatchet and left a message with her, but she may have had difficulty understanding me, it wasn't a very good line. My meeting with Colin Bucknall was pure coincidence—he'd gone into town to buy some paints and brushes. What could I do but accept when he offered me a lift home?'

Neil was full of remorse at once. 'I always seem to be

saying sorry,' he said with contrition, 'but I do mean it. I'm sorry to have blasted off at you, especially after you've been through such a hell of a time. As for poor Mrs H—she was in no condition to take messages last night. I found her in a state of collapse.'

Lesley gave a cry. 'Her heart?'

'Fortunately no, though she was barely conscious. She told me later that she came over very giddy and lost her balance. She also complained of nausea and loud noises in her ears. I was certain of the diagnosis by then, but I wanted it confirmed, so I got her into hospital right away. She was seen by Phillips, the ear, nose and throat specialist, this morning, and he's confirmed Ménière's Disease.'

This was something Lesley had not thought of. 'I'm afraid I haven't seen many cases of Ménière's Disease, I should have consulted my medical books when I had my doubts. Poor Mrs Hatchet!'

'I have no excuse for missing it,' said Neil, impatient with himself. 'You told me she suffered from vertigo, I'd noticed her growing deafness myself—I should have put two and two together. I think my grandmother was right about shoemakers' children and doctors' wives, only in this case it was a doctor's housekeeper.'

'What happens now?' asked Lesley anxiously.

'She'll be kept in hospital under observation for a few days. Treatment has already started—a course of drugs to combat the vertigo, which is the most distressing symptom. As for the deafness, some cases have been known to recover, so we can only hope for the best.'

'But do you know the cause? Has Mrs Hatchet been able to give you any information?'

He took hold of her arm just above the elbow and began to walk her towards the gate to the cottage garden. 'I can only make a guess. She told me she had middle-ear disease as a child which resulted in a perforated eardrum. Her mother treated it by soaking a piece of flannel in hot camphorated oil and applying it to the ear. It eased the pain, but who knows—some chronic infection might have been lying dormant all these years and something has triggered it off. Now we've isolated the ailment we'll know best how to treat it. As soon as Mrs H is out of hospital I'm packing her off on holiday somewhere. I've got to make it up to her somehow.'

They had reached the front door. Neil gave Lesley a lopsided smile that sent her pulses fluttering. 'Forgive me for talking shop. I haven't even given you time to get back into harness before getting at you! Fran will be glad to see you back, she's missed you. Jan's been with her all afternoon and I've been invited to supper, so it will be a little reunion get-together.'

His tone was lighthearted now, his eyes friendly, but this wasn't the same man who had kissed her. There was a certain detachment about him, and she didn't believe it was because he had caught her with Colin Bucknall. She couldn't mean that much to him.

CHAPTER EIGHT

It was Saturday June the fourth, and Lesley stretched lazily in bed, enjoying her lie-in. She felt she had earned this respite, for she had returned from London straight into the deep end of a minor epidemic of sore throats. Neil had considered it serious enough to order the taking of throat swabs of all known cases, and isolating others who might have been in contact. As the cause had been identified as a virus the treatment had been bed-rest, gargles, and a mouth-wash when necessary to restrain coughing. There had been no new cases for two days and those who had been worst infected were now on the way to recovery. For this reason the evening's party was being looked forward to as much as a tonic as anything else.

Lesley had planned to go to Roshaven that afternoon to have her hair done, because though Karen had been very complimentary about it it now needed expert attention. Also there was a new dress to buy and, more important still, a birthday present for Neil.

Lesley had barely exchanged a word with him since being back that hadn't referred to work, and she was hoping the evening would see a lowering of the barrier that had grown insidiously between them. She determined to make herself as attractive as possible for the party, and wasn't above practising a few feminine wiles to obtain her ends. She had discovered in the short time she had been at Trevaise that her old habit of retiring into her shell when the pressures began to mount would get her nowhere.

The first three-quarters of an hour in Roshaven was spent in looking for something suitable for Neil. She was about to give up and go for something mundane like toilet things, when passing an antique shop she spotted among some flyblown pictures an etching of a nineteenth-century tea clipper in full sail—one of the tall ships that had brought prosperity to Falmouth in the middle of the last century. The etching was in good condition and the frame looked new. Lesley came out of the shop quite pleased with her purchase.

Next to the dress shop—the shop where she had bought her grey silk blouse—she had her mind set on a silk dress with batwings sleeves. Again she was in luck. They had one dress only in her size, in a soft golden shade that exactly matched the colour of her hair. By this time she felt so confident that the tide of luck was running in her favour that she started looking for a pair of golden sandals to go with the dress, and got those at the second shoe shop she tried. By the time she came out of the hairdressing salon she felt she was coasting along on air. Her ears still tingled with the compliments the middle-aged proprietor had paid her. She knew a lot of what he said was professional chat, but she could see for herself the improvement in her hair. He was a wizard with a pair of scissors, and just by cutting alone he had coaxed back the curls she hadn't seen since her childhood days.

Lesley alighted from Dave's bus at the harbourside and walked to Cliff Cottage along the track by the shore, enjoying the salty tang in the slight breeze that gently ruffled her newly set hair. The sun glinted on the wings of the gulls high above her as they floated on the thermals, giving them a metallic sheen, and out on the horizon she could see the long low shape of a coaster as it nosed into the bay.

She looked at her watch as the cottage came into sight; she had just two hours before the evening celebrations got under way. Fran, Chris, Jan and Neil were already at the Club preparing the rooms for the party, and Chris had promised to call back for her about seven.

As she opened the gate and stepped down into the cottage garden a figure moved out of the shadow of the shrubbery. It was a girl—not anyone Lesley instantly recognised. 'Dr Colman,' the girl sounded edgy. 'Do you remember me?'

Lesley stared. Where could she have seen this girl before? Not as a patient, she was certain of that. Yet there was something vaguely familiar in the colour of her hair and in the pale green eyes.

'We met just the once, at St Bede's,' the girl went on. 'I was with Neil Rodway. I remembered your name tag—Dr Colman. I remarked on it at the time.'

A wave of embarrassment went over Lesley. She always tried to suppress the memory of that fateful encounter in the corridor of St Bede's. This was Vita Barry! She found it hard to believe, for without any make-up the girl's face looked oddly naked. She was a faded version of her former vivacious self, and there was something hangdog about her expression too.

'You don't recognise me,' she said sullenly. 'I didn't expect you to. I've been ill—but I'm feeling better now, I shall be all right once I get my make-up on again. I haven't felt like it these last few weeks. I wanted to see you especially—I've been waiting here over an hour.'

Lesley was conscious of a feeling of uneasiness. 'If it's for professional reasons I'm afraid I can't see you now. This is a private house and has no medical facilities. I'm afraid the surgery isn't open on Saturdays, but I could see you first thing on Monday.'

The girl shrugged. 'I'm only staying down here for a few days, with my cousin; I've got to go back to London on Monday. Look, Dr Colman, it's only to talk. I know what's wrong with me, I only want advice.'

'But you know Dr Rodway. Why didn't you contact him?'

The girl narrowed her eyes and there was a fleeting slyness about them. 'Because I'd rather talk to a woman doctor. My cousin told me about Neil's new assistant and what with the name and the description, I put two and two together.'

Yes, she'd be good at that, Lesley thought as she inserted her key in the lock. Vita had that knowing look about her. She showed the girl into the sitting-room, and when she returned after leaving her shopping in the kitchen she found she had seated herself with her back to the window so that her face was in shadow.

'I'm afraid I can only give you twenty minutes,' said Lesley as she sat opposite her. 'I'm going out this evening.'

Vita smirked. 'It won't take two minutes to say what I have to say. I'm pregnant, and I want to know how to get rid of it.'

Lesley had faced similar situations before. She had talked to women who had wanted to terminate their pregnancies because of lack of money, or overcrowding, or an already large family; perhaps because of domestic problems—but never had she come across such callousness, such a blunt lack of feeling. She thought of Fran and could hardly contain her anger.

'Have you thought this over? Have you discussed it with—' a quick glance at the girl's left hand, 'your boy-friend?'

'There isn't a boy-friend—I haven't even any family, that's why I've got to get rid of it.'

Lesley couldn't even feel pity, there was something so hard and unnatural about the girl's attitude.

'And I've got a job I like,' the girl went on. 'In an advertising agency. The prospects are good, so I don't want to spoil my chances by going through with this.'

'I don't think I can advise you,' said Lesely after a pause. 'And in any case, I don't think you're emotionally fit to make such a decision at the present time.'

'I've got to do something pretty damn quick,' Vita retorted sharply. 'I'm more than three months gone, it'll be dangerous to put if off any longer. I was hoping you could do something for me while I was down here so that they wouldn't know in London, where I live.'

'I'm afraid you expect the impossible. Even if I could do something, as you suggest, do you honestly believe it would be all over by Monday?'

'If I had a good reason I could extend my holiday.'

'It's out of the question,' said Lesley, suddenly losing patience. 'I have no power to arrange an abortion, that would be for a specialist to decide, and then you'd have to have a good reason. Look here—' she softened her tone, 'go to see Dr Rodway, go tomorrow, he'll be home then. You knew him very well once, he could give you better advice than I can.'

Again that crafty expression settled on the girl's face.

'Oh yes, I knew him very well once—too well. That's the reason I won't go to him. You see, he could well be the father!'

At those words Lesley felt shock waves race through her. When she finally found her voice her words sounded far away and toneless, as if in a dream. No, not a dream—a nightmare. 'Do—do you realise the seriousness of your allegation?'

The girl gave a short ugly laugh. Such venom glittered in her pale eyes that Lesley was totally convinced that her sudden appearance had been cunningly thought out. To break such news as this, and to herself in particular, was part of planned revenge on Neil. For throwing her over? Only a tortuous mind could work out such a ploy. For instance, she must have had her pregnancy confirmed or she wouldn't have sounded so confident about it—why then had she not sought advice about an abortion from the same hospital? No, her intention had been to return to Cornwall and cause as much mischief as she could.

Lesley could almost pity the girl for being a victim of so much malice and hatred, but she put that emotion aside. She had suddenly remembered Fran's words once spoken in desperation: 'Some day a girl will walk into the surgery to say she's pregnant and wanting someone to adopt her baby, and I shall be waiting'—something like that. It would be a gamble Lesley was willing to risk to save Neil's child, because she was convinced in her mind that Neil was the father.

'Have you thought about adoption?' she asked as casually as she could manage. She didn't want Vita to suspect the latent urgency, she might be perverse enough to destroy anything anybody else wanted. 'I know a couple who would be willing to adopt, and they would see you were well looked after during your pregnancy.'

'Yes, I've thought of it,' Vita admitted sullenly. 'But why should I go through all that hassle to give somebody else the benefit? And what about the expense? I only have my salary.'

Lesley chose her words carefully. 'I know a couple who would be happy to adopt a child. They're quite comfortably off, they would see you were well provided for.' She could see the other girl's mind working—asking, 'What is there in this for me?'

'Am I allowed to know who they are?'

'Of course, I can't stop you knowing that. Dr and Mrs Watling.'

The pale eyes in their nest of colourless lashes widened, then glinted with a malicious triumph. 'Not that Fran Watling! That stuck-up—' the girl interrupted herself to give another toneless laugh. 'What a twist of fate—she couldn't stand me, and she showed it. He was nice, though.' She got up and began to move restlessly about the room, as if she could think better that way. 'All right, I agree, but only on one condition. Nobody must know anything about me. Neither the Watlings nor Neil—especially not Neil. I don't care who you say the baby is as long as you don't mention my name. And I want you to act as go-between. I'll give you my address and the name of my bank, and you can make the necessary arrangements. Is that agreed?'

Lesley nodded. She didn't see what else she could do—Vita held all the trumps. The girl took a card from her bag and gave it to her. It was a business card belonging to the advertising agency, and on the back, handwritten, was Vita's home address.

'Right, then,' she said, slinging her bag over her shoulder. 'I'll wait now until I hear from you—the ball's in your court.'

Lesley followed her to the door, feeling she should offer refreshments but knowing she had to get Vita out of her sight before her feeling of numbness wore off. 'I'm still not happy about the ethics of all this,' she said.

'Couldn't I discuss it with my colleagues—mention your name, but nothing else?'

'No!' Both the voice and expression were adamant. 'Neil Rodway mustn't know a thing about this. If you as much as drop a hint, you'll never see or hear from me again!'

Lesley looked at her with compassion. Suddenly she thought she knew what was wrong. 'You must love him very much,' she said softly.

Tears welled unexpectedly in the pale eyes. 'I'll get over it,' Vita said with a false bravado. The moment of weakness passed, the hardness returned to her voice. 'I'll be hearing from you then and you'd better make it soon!'

Lesley prepared for the evening in a state of insensibility. Like an automaton she went through the motions of showering and changing and applying make-up, then stared at the all-gold figure in her looking-glass as if it were a stranger.

Chris came early. He looked stunned when he saw her—was her anguish so plain for everyone to see? 'Don't you think you'd better—' he started to say, but she cut him short.

'Don't worry about me—I'm all right. Come along, let's go.'

He said nothing more but drove the short way to the Yacht Club in an embarrassed silence. Only when they arrived did Lesley understand the true reason for his discomfiture. It was her clothes, not her expression, that had surprised him. Everybody else was in smart but practical sailing kit—and she had turned up as if for a state banquet! Fran hustled her off to the ladies' cloakroom.

'My God, Lesley, why are you all dressed up? Had

you forgotten we're going over Neil's boat, and that he's taking us for a sail later? I thought you took that for granted.'

'Neil said a party, so I dressed for a party,' said Lesley woodenly.

Fran stared at her. 'Are you all right Lesley? You look—well, rather odd.'

'Very odd, I should think,' said Lesley, deliberately misunderstanding. 'I'd better slip away—is there another door—?'

On her guard because of Lesley's manner, Fran said, 'Oh no, you don't! I know you—once you escape you won't come back. What would Neil think—that you don't like the company!'

'I only want to change!'

Fran chuckled. 'I'm beginning to see the funny side of it. What an entrance!—you swept in like some goddess from the Golden Age, and no pun intended. No, don't change, you look stunning, and why not be different —there's no law against it. Go out there and floor the whole lot of them!'

'Don't try to console me, I know I've made an idiot of myself.'

Yet Lesley took Fran's words to heart and went back to the crowded lounge with her head high, a shimmering golden figure from the crown of her head to the toes of sandals. She couldn't miss the admiration in the eyes of the men, and even envy in some of the women's, but it was small consolation. Vita's poison was beginning to work, and her numbness was giving way to an inconsolable ache.

Neil too was speechless when he first saw her. His eyes lit up like a blue flame and the faintest of smiles played about his mouth, yet there was admiration and even respect in his glance, which was not lost on his companion. This was a girl in her middle twenties who clung possessively to his arm. She was dark, nothing remarkable about her looks, with the exception of her eyes, which though a violet-blue had pupils so extended that they made the irises look black—a sign of sexuality which was apparent in every movement of her body.

Neil introduced her. 'Lesley, your predecessor, Dr Price—now Mrs Dorinda Parr.'

They eyed each other guardedly, each seeing in the other the antithesis of themselves. Among that company in their plain slacks and sweaters Dorinda Parr looked just as incongruous as Lesley, in her black velvet pants and silver lurex top.

'And how have you settled down in a country practice after the challenge of London?' Dorinda drawled her words in a husky, sexy voice.

Lesley had no wish to be drawn into the pros and cons of country versus town medicine, any more than she wanted to go on standing there feeling the eyes of the room upon her. She made her excuses to leave and seeing Moira, the District Nurse, going round with a tray of sherry, went after her. She needed a drink.

Moira Howard looked fetching in a dogs'-tooth trouser suit. Her cheeks were flushed with excitement, her eyes sparkled, she looked pretty. She was the only one who didn't react with surprise at the sight of Lesley, she just said in her calm way, 'You look an absolute dream,' and she was being sincere.

Fran joined them. 'Dorinda's in great form tonight,' she said with a reluctant admiration. The three of them followed Neil's progress as he greeted each guest, his one-time assistant in her role as self-imposed hostess glued to his side.

Lesley looked away. She felt she could never trust Neil again. It was no good trying to be rational—trying to tell herself she had no right to judge him, that his affairs were no concern of hers and that his relationship with Vita was over before she herself had even met him. In spite of his arrogance and quick temper (which he would be the first to admit) she had grown to like and respect him. Because of his compassion and fairmindedness—and yes, to be honest, his striking good looks—she had fallen deeply in love with him. And now because he had been shown up as a flawed man (not because of his affairs, but how could he have been attracted to a girl like Vita—empty-headed, shallow and vindictive?—That showed his lack of discrimination) it did not mean she would stop loving him. It would only be that much harder to bear.

Her thoughts were shattered by a laugh she instantly recognised; the girl in the moonlit garden of Carn House had laughed in the same way. Turning, she saw it was Dorinda, looking up at Neil and still laughing, her head in the same pose that Lesley had seen silhouetted against the moon-whitened tree. So she was the mystery girl—and what about her husband? Where was he? Lesley felt too sick at heart to care.

'Poor Moira,' said Fran suddenly, making Lesley realise the nurse was no longer with them. She had gone back to the bar to replenish her tray of sherry. She was there now, awaiting attention, and all the time her eyes were on Neil.

Lesley echoed, 'What do you mean—poor Moira?' But she already knew.

'Surely you've noticed—surely you've seen the way her eyes follow Neil everywhere? She wears her heart on her sleeve—that's why I said poor Moira.'

Lesley felt a tightening of the invisible band that had gripped her all evening. 'Do you think Neil realises?' she asked faintly.

'Oh yes, Neil suspects all right, but he's never let on. Haven't you noticed how gentle he is with her—how he never shouts at her or loses his temper?

'You mean he loves her?'

'Lesley, wake up! If he loved her would he be parading that other woman around in front of her? No, he doesn't love her. Neil doesn't show his love by tenderness—far from it. Have you ever seen him gentle with young Jan—and he worships her!' Fran's expression changed and her voice deepened with regret. 'Neil hasn't been in love for years. Sometimes I think he never will again.'

'Again—you said again. You mean he was once?'

Fran stared reflectively into the middle distance. 'There was someone once Neil wanted to marry, but she chose someone else. Then she was killed—so in a sense he lost her twice over. He was bitter for a long time—I think he's frightened to let himself fall in love again. Dorinda tried her hardest to become Mrs Rodway, though she was already engaged when she joined the practice—but Neil doesn't poach other men's property.'

'Where is her husband?' asked Lesley. 'Not here tonight?'

'No—he's in Nigeria on a six months' contract. He's a civil engineer and in charge of a road-building scheme there. Their home is in St Ives. Don't you remember Jan went there for her Easter holidays?'

Just as if she was aware they were talking about her, Jan suddenly erupted from the inner room. Her eyes widened to their fullest extent when she saw Lesley. 'Wow!' she exclaimed.

Her eyes began to dance with merriment. 'I can't wait to see you climbing into *Seawife* in that outfit! I thought Dorinda had gone over the top—but you've pushed her down into second place!' She wasn't being impertinent, just stating a fact.

Lesley felt she had been reprieved when supper was announced, until she found herself sharing a table with Chris, Fran, Moira, Neil and Dorinda. Jan went off to join a noisy young crowd of cadets, all in their teens and mostly boys. They were the junior members of the Yacht Club and, like Jan, owned their own sailing dinghies. Lesley ate what was put before her in a mechanical way, joining in the conversation as little as possible. Her silence went unnoticed, nobody stood much chance against Dorinda, who was a compulsive talker. She had recently taken a locum job in a north Cornwall town and went into great detail about her duties, which according to her were much more arduous than anything she had encountered at Trevaise. Once Neil caught Lesley's eye and called down the table, 'You ran away before you gave me the chance to thank you for my present. You must be a witch, knowing what to give me—there's nothing I wanted more, a rare print of one of the old clippers. Where did you find it?'

Lesley started to explain, but Dorinda broke in, twisting in her chair so that she could look Neil full in the face. 'I haven't given you my present yet, Neil—but you'll have to collect it. I won't tell you what it is, but you won't be disappointed.' There was no misunderstanding the invitation behind her words. Lesley blushed for her and was gratified to see Neil looked annoyed. When Dorinda went to help herself to more wine he put the bottle out of her reach. 'You've had quite enough,' he said curtly.

At last the meal ground to its finish and they drifted

back to the main lounge. Someone had brought a cassette player and the younger ones were already dancing. Fran and Chris were soon on the floor joining in with gusto. Neil came across to Lesley.

'It's not the right kind of music, but I think we can dance to it. Care to try?'

He didn't give her any choice but pulled her out into the middle of the dancers. 'But I can't dance. I don't know how,' protested Lesley.

'Neither do I, but we can walk in time to the music.' Which was what they did, in such style and looking such a handsome pair that many admiring eyes followed them around the room.

'You look ravishing—good enough to eat,' Neil said once, his mouth close to her ear. His hand was warm and firm on hers and she could feel the steady beat of his pulse—her own was racing. She knew he was flirting with her and wondered how many more conquests he wanted to make. He had Dorinda and Moira and Vita grovelling at his feet—did he want her too? No—she wasn't being fair—only Dorinda was grovelling and she would regret it in the sober light of morning. But why this unusual tenderness on his part towards her, especially after his offhand manner of the past few days? Then she went hot, remembering what Fran had said about his feelings towards Moira—that he was gentle with her because he knew how she felt about him. Had she, Lesley, given herself away so completely too? She stiffened in his arms and took up his words, saying acidly, 'I'm also lacking in imagination, otherwise I wouldn't have come dressed like this to a sailing party.'

His lips curled into a smile and she caught the gleam in his eyes before he half-closed them as if enjoying some private joke. 'And robbed us all of the chance to see you like a vision? It's been a revelation to me. I believe you're a woman of mystery.'

'I'm a woman who's done herself out of the chance of seeing over your boat,' she retorted, and at that he laughed aloud.

'Oh, you're not going to get out of that. We keep spare oilskins and deck shoes in the locker-room here, we'll rig you out. We'll have to find something for Dorinda too.'

'Did I hear my name being mentioned?' Dorinda had reappeared at their elbow; she had disappeared after supper to refresh her make-up. The pupils of her violet eyes glittered large and black in the spotlights as she leant against Neil, putting her head on his shoulder.

It gave Lesley the chance to slip away. Neil's nearness was too much of a torment and she wanted to escape —but the evening charade wasn't over for her just yet. There was still the trip out by dinghy to *Seawife* on its mooring in the creek. Jan took Lesley in hand; they were in the first boat-load to leave. Not all the guests were joining the boarding party, some wanted to stay and dance—some just to prop up the bar and talk. Only the keenest yachtsmen wanted to inspect *Seawife*'s improvements—later that evening when the moon was up a flotilla of boats would head upstream for a midnight picnic on a small island and, for a few of the hardiest, a moonlight swim.

Lesley followed Jan's progress over Neil's boat, not being allowed to miss a single item, though a lot of what Jan said went over her head. She tried to show an intelligent interest and she was impressed by the roominess of the yacht and how every inch of space was utilised. There were six berths, two in the forecabin, two in the saloon and two aft in a small cabin separated from the saloon by a roomy cockpit. The auxiliary engine was sited here, and its broad cover made a convenient cocktail bar for those guests who had brought refreshments with them. There was also a small galley and toilet compartment as well as numerous lockers for the storage of clothes and provisions. Even Lesley, who had never set foot on a boat before, felt some inborn sense of adventure at the thought of a trip in her, but not tonight. It was becoming more and more difficult to keep up her pretence of bonhomie, the effort was draining her.

Jan wouldn't give up, though she was hollow-eyed from want of sleep; she was jabbering away about mainsheets and genoa sheets when Lesley overheard Dorinda, who was nearby with Neil, say laughingly, 'Poor Dr Colman! I expect she thinks sheets are things you put on beds.'

'She knows better than that,' Neil answered grimly. He took Dorinda by her shoulders and pushed her into the empty saloon. Lesley turned to Jan.

'Now tell me—just what are sheets?'

'They're what you landlubbers call ropes—the word rope is never used on a boat. To put it simply—ropes that are used to moor craft are called warps. Ropes used for general use are called lines. Ropes which control the set of the sails are known as sheets, and the ropes which are used for hoisting the sails are called halliards. They're sometimes made of wire.'

Lesley looked blank. 'How can I be expected to remember that?'

Jan grinned. 'What about you learning to sail—I'll teach you. You did think about it once. My little dinghy is only half the size of *Seawife*'s dinghy, and hasn't an outboard, only a lug-sail, but I get buckets of fun with her. Go on, Lesley, say yes! We could have a good time together this summer.'

'I thought you were going off to Hong Kong?'

Jan shook her head. 'That's off. Mummy and Dad are moving on to Japan for three months—something to do with Dad's job. I'm not sorry—there's so much doing here in Trevaise in the summer. With my little *Pipit* we can go exploring all the tiny little creeks that the *Seawife* can't negotiate. I bet I could soon teach you to sail.'

From the saloon Lesley could hear Dorinda's husky laughter—Neil's deep voice, then sudden silence, and in her imagination she could see them locked again in embrace. 'If you can't beat them, join them,' she told herself in a rush of false optimism. To Jan she said, 'Right, I'll take you up on that.'

Towards midnight when preparations were being made for the trip to the island Lesley began to look around for an excuse to leave. She didn't have to look far. Jan was almost asleep on her feet; she pointed her out to Fran. Fran also wanted to get away. Chris had been called out twice that evening and looked tired. She told Neil they were going home and would take Jan with them, and if he was disappointed he didn't show it. Since they had returned from *Seawife* he had stayed in the bar talking to other sailing enthusiasts, with Dorinda by his side. He did walk outside to see them off, and sniffed appreciatively at the fresh air.

'What a fug in there! I shall be glad to get out on the water.'

Chris looked up at the star-crested sky. 'There's no wind—you won't be hoisting sails tonight.'

'Wouldn't have bothered anyway, it's only a short run up to the island. It's the swim that's the main attraction.'

'I hope you've remembered your swimsuits,' Fran

remarked as she got into the back of the car alongside Jan and Lesley.

Dorinda had followed Neil. They could see her silver top shimmering in the half-light. 'Who said anything about swimsuits—it will be too dark to see anyway.' Her voice was husky with innuendo.

'It's about time Stephen Parr returned to keep his wife in order,' grunted Chris as he slammed the car into gear.

Jan was sleeping at Cliff Cottage for that night. As Lesley helped her into bed—the child was too tired to undress herself—she heard the phone shrilling in the hall below and guessed it was for Chris. The welcome aroma of freshly made coffee greeted her back in the kitchen.

'That was poor old Mrs Bettany,' said Fran as she placed coffee and biscuits on the table. 'Having another of her asthmatic attacks. Chris has taken her some anti-histamine tablets, but he'll stay with her for a while. She gets into a panic at such times, and her heart is a bit dicky.'

'I wanted the chance to have a talk with you,' said Lesley, staring into her cup. She looked up to see Fran's eyes on her, focused with a kind of dread.

'It's bad news, isn't it? I knew there was something wrong by your manner this evening. You covered it up well—but every now and then you had a look on your face that frightened me.'

'It's not bad news, quite the contrary. Sit down, Fran, I can't talk to you while you're hovering over me like that.'

Fran sat opposite resting both hands on the table. Lesley gave her a wan smile. 'Do you remember telling me that you believed one day a girl would come to the surgery saying she was pregnant and wanting somebody to adopt her baby?'

Fran turned pale. She leant forward, her hands clasped together. 'Don't play with me, Lesley—come to the point!'

'Well, such a girl did turn up this afternoon—not to the surgery, but here. For reasons I won't go into she doesn't want to keep the baby and she's quite agreeable to have it adopted. But she insists on keeping anonymous and wants me to act as go-between. I said I would discuss it with you.'

Fran said nothing, but her face suddenly crumpled and tears spilled silently out of her eyes. Lesley had never seen her cry before and sometimes wondered if she was capable of tears; now she felt a wrench at her heartstrings to see such a release of pent-up longing. 'I'm worried about the ethics of it,' she went on. 'I think all adoptions should go through the official channels, but then you might have to wait your turn. There are so many childless couples anxious to adopt these days and so few children available for adoption.'

'But this one is mine—mine!' cried Fran, her voice rising with agitation. 'And I won't let any official take it from me! It wasn't just fate that brought this particular girl to this particular house—it was foreordained. You can make any arrangements with the mother you like, I know Chris will agree to that too. He wants a baby as much as I do. Oh, Lesley, I can't believe this has really happened!' Fran sighed. 'I'll wake up tomorrow and find it was all a dream. Tell me everything—tell me I'm not just imagining this conversation!'

'It all happened,' said Lesley. Her voice sounded tired, but Fran put that down to the lateness of the hour. She listened without interrupting as Lesley went over the events of the afternoon.

'And I'm not to know the girl's name or where she comes from or anything about her?'

'That's her condition.'

Fran shrugged in a happy carefree manner. 'I don't care, of course—it's the baby that matters, nothing else. But—but I suppose it's too much to hope there's a Cornish connection.'

Lesley smiled bleakly. 'The father is Cornish,' she said.

CHAPTER NINE

WORK had always been the antidote for Lesley when she was troubled about anything, and work she had in plenty for the next two weeks.

Mrs Hatchet had returned home the Monday following the Yacht Club party, but not for long. In spite of her protests Neil had driven her to Penzance to spend two weeks convalescing with her sister. The hospital treatment for the Ménière's Disease had been effective; the vertigo was now under control and her hearing improved. She looked a different person, far more relaxed, and all signs of strain gone from her face. For the first time she admitted how frightened she had been by the constant buzzing in her ears and the sudden attacks of giddiness had depressed her. Life was going to be much easier for Mrs Hatchet in future—and for those around her!

And then the hospital sent for Mrs Bourne. An X-ray diagnosis had revealed that the kneecap had been virtually eaten away by her arthritis and removal of the broken parts was necessary. Neil himself performed this operation, and he asked Lesley to assist him.

She was flattered by his offer, but the very fact that he had made it emphasised that he expected her to return to St Bede's to take up a career in surgery. She had already written to James telling him she was interested in the surgical house job that was becoming vacant in September, and as she knew Neil and James were in touch, especially since the birth of the twins, it was more than likely James had passed back this information to him.

She now had to face up to the fact that her time at Trevaise was running out. She tried to look upon it as an interlude—in some ways a pleasant holiday, or romantically—a Cornish rhapsody. The idea that she had allowed herself to fall in love with a man who had no interest in her outside the surgery only stressed the need to get back to London and reality.

But standing by the operating table, watching Neil at work, made her realise even more the powerful attraction he exerted over her. She admired expertise in whatever form, and Neil was an expert at his work. Only after the damaged knee had been incised was the extent of the damage to the patella apparent. The cartilage had worn away completely and the bone had degenerated into several small pieces which had to be picked out separately. Walking for the patient must have been agony. Swiftly and efficiently the wound was stitched and plaster-impregnated bandages wound around the leg from ankle to thigh, then Mrs Bourne was wheeled into the recovery room. Later, when she had been taken back to her ward, Lesley went along to visit her.

She was still drowsy from the anaesthetic and complaining of the thirst that was tormenting her. But fluids were forbidden for several hours, so Lesley fetched the staff nurse and asked her to give Mrs Bourne a mouthwash which at least would alleviate some of the dryness. When next Lesley visited the ward, two days later, she saw a remarkable improvement.

Mrs Bourne was out of bed sitting in one chair, her plastered leg supported on another. Colour had returned to her face and she was smiling. On her locker was a bowl of red roses.

'I see you have a secret admirer,' Lesley teased.

A blissful look spread over Mrs Bourne's placid features. 'From my boy Steve—he sold a car. He's a good boy at heart, Doctor.' This last Lesley took as a mild rebuke, and well deserved. She would have to amend her opinion of young Steve Bourne.

'And how do you feel in yourself?' she asked. 'You look well.'

'I'm fine, Doctor, only this old leg feels as if it weighs a ton. Dr Rodway says I can have the plaster off in ten days, and then some physiotherapy treatment, and perhaps I'll have to walk with a stick for a bit, but he promises me I'll be walking without a limp by the time my husband gets home. He's a lovely man!' And Lesley knew she wasn't referring to her husband.

The arrangements with Vita were now completed. She didn't answer Lesley's letter telling her that Fran and Chris would abide by her conditions, so it was obvious she was quite happy with the allowance being made to her via her bank. As Lesley had expected, Neil condemned the whole plan and advised Chris to have nothing to do with such a hole-and-corner arrangement, but there he came up against fanatical opposition from Fran, who saw this as her last chance for a child.

And it was worth the slight uneasiness everyone felt to see the change in Fran. She blossomed out like a fulfilled woman. Her bouts of depression ceased—there were no longer angry silences, no bursts of frantic activity, as if she dared not risk the chance of having time to think. This new contented Fran who went about humming to herself was a revelation both to Lesley and Chris, and as Chris once remarked, 'Fran had all the symptoms of a happy pregnancy.'

One outcome of Vita's disclosure was that Lesley got in touch with Colin Bucknall and told him she had changed her mind about having her portrait painted and arranged to have sittings. Why had she changed her mind? She asked herself that many times without getting a satisfactory answer. Because it was a woman's prerogative?—no, she wasn't that type of a woman. To get her own back on Neil?—she wasn't that type of person either. Perhaps, she decided finally, she wanted in some small way to leave her mark on Trevaise. It would be a lasting memorial to a foolish woman who had spent one short summer there and lost her heart not only to a place but also a man.

She started her sittings in July. Colin had wanted to paint her in skirt and anorak, on the pier surrounded by seagulls as he had first seen her, but she wouldn't have that. She wanted to be painted in her gold dress, she might as well get some benefit from it, and when Colin saw her in it he readily agreed.

'It's perfect,' he said. 'I'll paint you sitting in the bow window at High Moors holding an armful of daffodils and I'll call it "Girl with Daffodils" instead of "Girl with Seagulls".'

She sat for him twice a week, once on her free afternoon and once during the weekend. Sometimes his aunt would sit in the room with them watching and sometimes putting in an unasked-for comment which Colin took in good part, but usually they were alone, and then Colin would talk. Lesley had no idea he could be so entertaining: he enthralled her with stories about other countries which had been mere words in an atlas but which he could bring vividly to life with a well-turned phrase.

He was very adamant about not letting her see how the work was progressing—he wanted her to wait until the picture was completed. Once towards the end of the sittings he touched on his private life. It came out quite by accident when he was describing his frustration when trying to paint a sunset in a village in Malaysia. 'It wouldn't come right,' he said. 'The nearer the Equator the more vivid the colours, but on canvas they looked garish and artificial. I was near despair, ready to give up—it was something I'd never attempted before and I wondered if it was beyond me—after all, I don't claim to be another Turner. Rosemary was with me, we were on our extended honeymoon, and she came and stood behind me. 'Don't paint as you see—paint as you feel,' she said. It sounds corny, but it worked for me. I miss her so much—not only her physical presence but her understanding—her wisdom. I look for them in other women, but so far—' and he shrugged his shoulders meaningfully.

'You couldn't have been married very long?' said Lesley, her voice expressing sympathy.

He stared out of heavy-lidded haunted eyes. 'Just six months. That trip to Malaysia was a spur-of-the-moment thing—we were due to return home. On our last day, we were driving back to our hotel when I turned the car over—God knows what happened. Rosemary was killed instantly—I crawled out of the wreckage with a broken ankle. I was ill for a long time after that and the fracture was neglected, and as you see, it's left me with a permanent limp. I've been told it's not too late to put right, but what's the odds—I've got used to it as it is, it doesn't worry me,' and he shrugged again.

'Do you mind if I give you some professional advice?'

He grinned sardonically. 'Go ahead, Doctor.'

'Get it seen to as quickly as possible—otherwise you may regret it later, especially if arthritis gets a hold. Do you know what I think? That you're treating your ankle as a form of punishment. You blame yourself for your wife's death—I don't say you enjoy being punished, but you feel you deserve it. Once you come to terms with your guilt, you'll be ready for treatment.'

Colin gave her a steady look. 'You're very perceptive. What do you know about guilt?'

'I had a guilt complex for years,' she answered earnestly, 'and it made me a very edgy person, not easy to get on with. I finally expunged my guilt this summer—and believe me, it was like throwing off a ton weight.'

He remarked dryly, 'I find it hard to believe you were ever guilty of anything.' He wiped his brushes clean, then threw a cover over the canvas. 'That's all for today, you can stretch now. One more sitting and this should be finished.' He paused, then spoke with his back half turned. 'I'm surprised you know so little about Rosemary. I would have expected Neil to mention her, considering how much he wanted to marry her himself.'

She felt the impact of his words like a blow. Colin's wife the girl Neil had once loved! Did this explain the open antagonism between the two men?

Colin was looking at her now. 'You seem stunned. You had no idea? Well, perhaps it's something he can't bring himself to talk about. I suppose it still rankles, being thrown over for me—he knew Rosemary first, they were practically engaged. I didn't influence her, she turned to me quite voluntarily.'

Lesley could understand that too—there was something about Colin that might appeal to the maternal instinct in some women. He looked as if he needed mothering.

Not all her spare time those summer evenings was spent at High Moors. Under Jan's supervision she was learning how to handle the little sailing dinghy, and making such good progress she was becoming quite smug about it. She had got over her fear of small boats, she loved the sensation of running before the wind, heeling over as they rounded the marker buoys and looking down to see two inches of freeboard and the water creaming under the bows. It didn't worry her now when the small boat keeled over, she had enough confidence in Jan's ability as a sailor, but for safety's sake Neil insisted on the wearing of lifejackets at all times, and they were forbidden to sail anywhere but in the creeks.

One fine evening they sailed up as far as *Seawife*'s mooring. There was a wide stretch of water here and Lesley was going to practise tacking. She was at the rudder and Jan held the mainsheet, and all went well until Lesley spotted Neil on the side deck of his yacht, leaning on the rail and grinning down at them; she then lost all concentration and rammed *Pipit* broadside into a nearby moored craft. There was no damage done except to Jan's dignity. The impact shot her on to the bottom of the boat, she let go of the mainsheet and the sail flapped in the breeze like washing on a clothesline. Neil enjoyed it hugely.

'Where are your L-plates, Doctor!' he yelled.

Jan took her place again, her face crimson with fury. She had been showing off too, basking in the glory of her pupil's new accomplishment. She couldn't understand why Lesley wasn't covered in confusion—*she* would have been in her place, but Lesley seemed to be struggling with inner laughter.

'Don't encourage him,' grated Jan between gritted teeth. 'He's bigheaded enough already. We'll never hear the last of this!'

But Neil was kind to them on this occasion; perhaps he remembered his own apprenticeship under old Bert Gooley's tutelage, for his only reference to sailing was to suggest they made up a party with Fran and Chris to sail up the River Fal the following Sunday. The trip had to be planned ahead; a colleague from a neighbouring practice was deputised to take emergency calls and Mrs Hatchet wanted notice about making four of her renowned Cornish pasties. They were the size of dinner plates and melted in the mouth. 'Meat and two veg wrapped in enjoyment,' Neil called them, warmed through in the yacht's cooker and followed by cheese and fruit, all washed down with a light wine—a lunch to be savoured after a long sail.

Lesley had a niggling fear that Dorinda might be asked to join the party, but Fran expressed surprise when she mentioned the possibility of this.

'Didn't you know—Dorinda flew off to Nigeria last week. I don't know whether anybody's been telling tales, but she had a phone call from her husband and the next day gave in her notice to the practice where she'd been doing a locum and off she went. Typical of Dorinda!'

'She must be very fond of her husband to go off like that.'

Fran gave a cynical laugh. 'Fond of his money, more like!'

Lesley awakened on the Sunday to look out on to a bay shrouded in mist. Her heart plummeted with disappointment, proving how much she had been looking forward to this outing, but the ever-optimistic Chris soon cheered her up.

'Nothing to worry about—it'll clear by mid-morning. It's only a low-lying mist, you can see the sky above. We won't be able to hoist the sail, though, there's no wind. Neil will have to rely on the engine.'

Even this was a novelty to Lesley. She had seen more and more pleasure boats crowd the small harbour as the season had advanced and had often envied the holidaymakers as she watched them chug out to sea. Now she was enjoying that same sensation.

Seawife ploughed through the waves with an ease that was deceptive; the water was so calm that movement was hardly noticeable. The two castles that guarded the entrance to Carrick Roads, the mile-wide stretch of water east of Falmouth, appeared out of the mist like twin beacons as they approached. They had been built by Henry VIII, Neil told her, as part of a coastal defence against a possible invasion by the French; Pendennis Castle high on its promontory by Falmouth harbour and St Mawes on the headland across the bay topped by a hill behind, and just as they passed them and sailed on into Carrick Roads the sun pierced the mist and the sea came alive in a shimmer of silver rivulets.

On then to King Harry Passage where the car ferry connected St Mawes to Falmouth, shortening the route to Truro. 'The same Henry?' queried Lesley.

'But not the same ferry,' said Neil with a laugh. 'There's a legend of him crossing the river at this point with his new wife Anne Boleyn. It's a nice story to tell the foreigners from up-along.'

'Foreigners from up-along?'

'That's what the Cornish call anybody from other parts of the country. We consider ourselves an independent sovereignty in these parts.'

The day had put him in a jokey mood. The yacht was heading up the river, passing a long line of redundant ships moored one behind the other. Sadly they reminded

Lesley of stranded whales, these giant iron and steel leviathans of the ocean washed up in the quiet anchorage of the Fal. Victims of the recession and a more technological age.

Fran, who had been quietly knitting, put her work away and suggested to Jan that they went off to the galley to make coffee. Chris followed in search of something stronger.

In spite of the steady hum of the engine it was oddly peaceful in the cockpit, particularly without Jan and her chattering tongue. On either side the heavily-wooded banks of the river rose high above them and though there were other boats on the move they sometimes had whole stretches of water to themselves.

Foreigners from up-along, Lesley repeated to herself, looking at Neil. He was three-quarters up-along himself, his only connection with Cornwall was through his grandmother. There was nothing remotely Celtic in his blond good looks. A Devon man perhaps, with a dash of long-ago Viking blood. Quietly she watched him, studying his face in profile as he stood at the wheel. The determined chin, the deceptively sweet curve of his mouth—deceptive because in anger it disappeared into a narrow thin line—the finely chiselled nose, the broad forehead, the plentiful dark gold hair, a little tousled now—she absorbed it all with eyes of longing.

He seemed unaware, even unaware of her presence —he was absorbed too much with the task in hand. Fran was right—*Seawife* was the only female he really cared about—and why not? He had a housekeeper to see to his creature comforts, and when he required feminine company there were many who would oblige. At the Yacht-Club party Dorinda had not been the only one to devour him with her eyes. He had no need for a lasting relationship with any particular woman.

'Something troubling you?' he asked suddenly, breaking into her thoughts, and she put on a brief smile.

'Not at all—just enjoying the atmosphere. It's all so lovely.'

'There's no room for passengers on this boat,' he answered casually. 'Come and take a turn at the wheel.'

Lesley was horrified by the idea. 'After what you saw me do to Jan's dinghy?'

'That's the reason. It's about time you had a lesson in steering. Come along, I'll guide you.'

When he used that tone of voice there was no denying him, so reluctantly she moved over to the wheel. He placed her hands in the correct position and kept his over them, guiding her by the merest pressure when they came to an obstacle. Her heart was pounding from the effect on her of his nearness—she only had to move her head and it rested against his shoulder. She stood like a ramrod, frightened to move, and Neil was quickly aware of this.

'You'll never make a helmsman standing as rigid as that. I can feel you, absolutely tense—relax, woman, relax!'

She wanted to shout, 'How can I relax with you standing so close?' but instead she quietly slipped her hands from beneath his and went back to her seat.

He stared. 'Is that it? You don't want to try any more?'

'I'm not in the mood.'

He frowned. He was disappointed in her and showed it. 'I just can't understand you at times,' he said. 'You're a very secret person. For instance, this adoption you've arranged for Fran and Chris—you got that buttoned up very nicely without a word to the rest of us. I'd be much happier about it if I knew who the mother was.'

The change in his manner put her on the defensive. 'I made a promise. I felt I owed the girl a certain loyalty.'

'And what about loyalty to Fran and Chris? Don't they count?'

'What a beastly thing to say! I did it for them in the first place, and they're quite satisfied with the arrangements.'

'You know as well as I do that Fran would agree to anything to get a child and Chris would agree to anything to make Fran happy. I only hope they have the sense to make this adoption legal when the time comes. I gather the mother is a friend of yours.'

'Not a friend exactly. I just happen to know her.'

'And you just happen to know the father too, Fran gave me to believe!' His tone was abrasive and it was on the point of Lesley's tongue to say it was no business of his when she realised how much it was. The enormity of her actions came home to her for the first time. What right had she to take it upon herself to interfere with the lives of others? She should not have made that bargain with Vita before talking it over with Fran and Chris first. She had allowed her heart to rule her head, and all because she had wanted to save the unborn child—because of the possibility that it could be Neil's. And what would his reaction be if he should ever find out that her decision alone had settled the fate of his own flesh and blood? She suddenly realised what a dangerous game she had been playing, and Neil's wrath, when it became known, as it surely would be, was something that didn't bear thinking about.

Fran appeared doing a balancing act with coffee on a tray. 'Sorry to take so long, the kettle took ages to boil. Where are we tying up, Neil?'

'The next inlet.'

'Right. I'll get Chris to light the oven, I hate fiddling with gas.'

A long lazy afternoon stretched before them. Chris got out his fishing line, Jan and Fran sunbathed on the cabin top, Neil offered to take Lesley for a row in the yacht's dinghy and when she refused went off on his own. For Lesley the light and the life had gone out of the day—all she wanted was to get back to Cliff Cottage to write to Vita pleading with her to let her break her promise and allow her to tell Fran and the others the baby's identity.

Towards late afternoon the temperature dropped and the two sunbathers put jackets over their suntops. A wind had arisen, blowing from the north-east, a wind that would send them scudding down the Fal towards the sea. Neil looked up at the burgee flapping at the mast-head with a smile of satisfaction. 'We'll have a fast run home,' he predicted.

Lesley went into the galley to help Fran to clear away the washed dishes, and felt very much a square peg in a round hole—there was a place for everything and every-thing in its place, but she didn't know where the places were, and it was quicker to let Fran get on with it rather than stop to show her.

It was the same when Neil gave the order to hoist the mainsail and she went forward to give assistance to Chris and Jan—she was only in the way again. This wasn't her world—she was, after all, just a passenger, and she returned to the cockpit to try to efface herself as much as possible. But for all her worry about the outcome of the adoption, she could not help thrilling at the sight of the mainsail being hoisted, and when, with the wind behind them, they went beating down river, the water singing under the bows, she felt a rush of blood to her heart and her pulse raced with excitement as she shared with Neil for one enchanted moment the joy of skimming over the water like a bird, and nurtured the wish that it could be just the two of them alone and sailing off together.

In Carrick Roads the wind was too strong even for the jib on its own and both sails were lowered. Jan was on the foredeck coiling the halliards and Lesley saw bother and sister exchange smiles; they were in their element.

'Back to the smelly old engine again,' said Jan as she jumped down into the cockpit.

'It's neither smelly nor old, but I grant you it's a poor second to sail,' said Neil. He tweaked Jan's nose. 'And this is going to be as red as a beacon tomorrow. I warned you about lying out in the sun!'

Neil and Jan came back to Cliff Cottage for supper. If Lesley appeared uncommunicative it went unnoticed, they were all suffering from a surfeit of sun and fresh air, and Jan practically fell asleep at the table. Neil took her home soon afterwards, and Chris and Fran went to bed. At last Lesley was free to write her letter to Vita. She slipped out to post it—it wouldn't be collected before eleven o'clock in the morning, but she would get no peace of mind until it was actually in the mail.

She had her final sitting with Colin the following week. He cleaned his brush for the last time, then called her over to see the finished portrait. She looked at it for a long time, not knowing whether to feel pleased with it or not—it wasn't at all what she had expected. Her face was in focus, the rest of her was a blur of gold that merged into the background—her hair, the dress, the flowers—different shades of yellow like patches of sunshine used as a means to highlight her face. That was a pale oval with enormous dark eyes that stared back at the viewer with an enigmatic expression.

'Why have you made me look so sad?' she asked in surprise.

'Sad!' He stood beside her, appraising his work with his head on one side. 'Not sad—thoughtful, perhaps.' He looked at her. 'You don't like it?'

'It doesn't really look like me, does it?'

She wished she hadn't said that, she saw she had hurt him.

'If you wanted a faithful likeness you could have had a coloured photograph. I don't paint like that. That is an impression of you as I see you, and everyone will see it differently. That's the criterion of a work of art—it should involve the viewer.'

The portrait went on exhibition in Roshaven at the end of August and made an immediate impact. There was so much publicity that a dealer from a Bond Street gallery came to see it and made Colin a good offer, but he said it was already sold. Nobody believed him, everybody thought he intended to keep the portrait for himself. Rumour already linked his name to Lesley's.

The only person who had nothing to say about the picture was Neil. Lesley had been prepared for that, knowing how he felt about Colin painting her, but it distressed her to think he cared so little for her he wouldn't trouble himself to see what the painting looked like.

Then came a wonderful surprise to ease her wounded feelings. Karen and James and the children came to stay at Carn House for a short holiday. Lesley could hardly believe that the two lusty three-month-old boys were the same tiny crimson scraps she had last seen in May. The old granite house on the hill was shaken out of its natural calm by the invasion of the three lively children, and Mrs Hatchet acquired a shadow in the form of four-year-old Amy, who followed her everywhere. Mrs Hatchet had enough wit to realise that it wasn't so much her company as the tin of chocolate chip biscuits she kept in the larder that was the attraction. But even cupboard-love meant something to a life that hadn't had a great deal of love, and when the day of departure came, the last toy retrieved, the last woolly plucked off the line, the last case bundled into the car, Lesley was surprised to see that the housekeeper's eyes were moist.

Another one who had been affected by the visit was Fran. She was always around the babies offering to help, always nursing one or other of the twins. 'That's what Colin should paint,' Lesley told herself one day as she watched Fran with David, though even Colin might find that look of utter felicity beyond him. Neil was watching too. 'Perhaps this adoption idea isn't such a bad one after all,' he conceded.

Vita hadn't answered her letter. But it was still August and she could be on holiday. It was on Lesley's mind to write again when at last Vita's answer arrived. Chris brought it up to her with her morning cup of tea.

She never did drink that tea. She read the first few lines, then got out of bed and went across to the window-seat, feeling the need of movement. Her hands were shaking a little as she read through the letter again. Vita had changed her mind about having her baby adopted. She had met somebody who wanted to marry her and wanted her to go ahead and have the baby. The letter rambled on:

. . . I came down to Trevaise with the idea of stirring up trouble—I wanted to get my own back on that toffee-nosed lot at the Yacht Club. They never did like me—but I don't feel vindictive any more and I'm sorry about some of the things I said, especially about Dr Rodway. I lied when I said he could have been the father of my child—there was never anything like that between us. I liked him ever such a lot, but he didn't think about me in that way at all. He only invited me to Carn House that time as company for his sister. He thought she was running wild and becoming too much of a tomboy and thought some feminine company would be good for her—but it didn't work out. I didn't fit in. I knew all along who the father of my baby is. He's someone where I used to work before I went to the advertising agency; married, of course, and now doesn't want to know. But it doesn't matter—I've met a good man now and I'm sure we'll make a go of it. He's been married before and has a little girl, and that's another reason he wants me to have this baby. And I want the baby myself too—I want a family, and I want to belong to a family, and that's something I've never had. So I'll always be very grateful to you for talking me out of having an abortion. You can tell the Watlings all about me now, I don't mind who knows—and tell them I'm sorry I've let them down. Tell them too I'll repay every penny I owe them . . .

Lesley let the letter fall out of her hand and stared blindly out of the window. Fran would have to be told. Neil would discover what she had believed of him. Either prospect chilled her to the marrow. She stooped and picked up the letter, then robot-like, went off to the bathroom to dress.

CHAPTER TEN

SOME strange compulsion caused Lesley to put on a new green linen dress, as if looking her best might help her to face the consequences of her actions. When she went downstairs she found Chris preparing breakfast. He had laid a tray with cereal, toast and marmalade and was just pouring coffee; he gave Lesley a cheerful grin.

'I'm spoiling Fran this morning. She's not feeling too great, got some kind of tummy upset, so doctor's orders are to stay in bed. Help yourself, Lesley.'

When he returned he was surprised to find that Lesley hadn't moved. Only then did he notice her strained expression.

He looked at the letter she was clutching. 'Anything up? Not bad news, I hope.'

She held the letter out to him and, puzzled, he took it and began to read, fleeting expressions of bewilderment and incredulity crossing his face. He looked up, frowning. 'I don't understand—what does this mean? Vita? How did she come to be writing to you? My God—I get it! It's *her* child! Lesley, what the hell is all this about?'

Lesley told him everything that had passed between Vita and herself that fateful afternoon in June—sparing him nothing. Chris heard her out without interrupting, his small intelligent eyes never wavering from her face. Only when she finished speaking did he sit down heavily at the table, rubbing his hand across his eyes. He read the letter through again, then flung it from him as if it were tainted.

'And you really believed her when she said Neil was the father of her child?'

Lesley nodded, too choked to speak.

He shook his head in disbelief. 'I can't begin to understand why she should accuse him. He was so good to her—he bothered about her, which was more than those cousins in Roshaven did. She landed herself on them when she lost her job in London, hoping to get a holiday job down here, but her relatives didn't encourage that idea. Somebody brought her along to one of the Yacht Club dances and she latched on to us—Fran, Neil and myself, I mean. I didn't see any harm in her, she was a friendly vivacious little thing, but Fran didn't take to her. As for Neil being sexually attracted to her—heavens, no!—she wasn't his type, and in any case, he looked upon her as a child, not much older than Jan. He tried to encourage the two to be friends, but Jan didn't like her either. In the end there was some kind of unpleasantness between Vita and her cousins and they told her to leave. That's when Neil invited her to Carn House until she got herself sorted out—typical of him, he was always one to help lame dogs. Perhaps Vita thought there was more to it—I don't know—I'm not very good at getting into a woman's mind,' and Chris gave a helpless shrug. 'Anyway, it didn't work out, and I remember Neil saying to me that he would have to find Vita a job, otherwise he'd have a permanent boarder on his hands. He knew one of the directors of the Selwyn Advertising Agency in Holborn and arranged an interview for her that time he came up to London and saw you. Well, there you have it.' Chris tapped the letter. 'He'll have to know about this.'

Lesley felt her legs buckle under her and sat down too.

'At the moment, Chris, I'm more concerned about

Fran. I haven't the courage to tell her. Will you?'

'I shall have to, won't I?' His shoulders sagged, in the past few minutes he looked as if he had aged. She saw that the skin around his eyes had lost colour. He stood up, pulling himself upright. 'I'll go up and face her now. What about Neil—you want me to tell him as well?'

The answer was in her eyes. She looked desperate.

It seemed such a short walk to the surgery that morning, though Lesley loitered, dreading the inevitable encounter with Neil. She had waited in the kitchen while Chris went up to Fran. She had waited for the expected cry of pain—a burst of hysterical tears—but there had been nothing but silence, and somehow she had found that more unnerving.

That day she had the afternoon free, so consequently her morning was fully booked, although the appointments began to ease off around midday. All morning she had been listening for the sound of Neil's step outside her door, though she knew it was his morning for a session at the hospital. Chris was also out visiting the branch surgeries and wouldn't be back until lunchtime. Her last patient had just gone, and stiff from sitting so long, she got up and went across to the window. The sea was like a sheet of blue silk, unruffled by turbulence—in sharp contrast to the state of her mind. A crab boat had just come into harbour and the gulls were gathering, tearing the stillness apart with their raucous cries. The house phone suddenly shrilled. Miss Pearson sounded breathless.

'I've got a young mother here, Doctor, in a terrible state. There's something wrong with her baby She's not registered with us, she's a visitor—'

'Send her in,' said Lesley quickly.

A young woman with an anxious expression came

bursting into the room, holding a restless and fretful baby. 'Oh, Doctor, I'm so worried!' she cried. 'Little Paul was perfectly all right yesterday, but he kept waking up crying during the night, and this morning I discovered he's covered all over in a rash. We're staying in a village miles inland and the car broke down or I would have been here earlier. It isn't measles, is it—he hasn't been inoculated yet.'

Lesley took the small child and examined him carefully, and only then did she allow herself the hint of a smile.

'First of all I can assure you it isn't measles or anything infectious. Are you feeding baby yourself?'

'Yes—but why? What's that got to do with it?'

'You don't give him any supplementary food?'

'Not yet, my own doctor says he's doing so well he doesn't need it. Please tell me what's wrong! I thought it was measles—there was measles at Julie's school last term. Julie's my little girl—'

Lesley began to reassure the distraught woman. 'It's an allergic rash—we call it urticaria—you may know it as nettlerash. You must have eaten something which has disagreed with your baby through the breast milk. Are you allergic to anything yourself? Did you eat anything yesterday that upset you?'

The woman screwed up her face in concentration. 'Just the usual boarding house food—good plain food, nothing fancy. Just a minute, though—' her face lightened. 'I remember I had a plate of mussels when we went out for a drink last night, and some bumps came up on my legs that itched for a bit, but I didn't think anything of it at the time. It couldn't be that, surely?'

'It most certainly could—you'll have to watch this young man in future and have him tested for allergies.

Consult your own doctor when you get home.' The child had stopped whimpering and was nuzzling against his mother's bodice. 'I think at the moment all he's interested in is his dinner, but I'll write you a prescription for some calomine lotion, that should help ease the irritation. The rash should begin to fade soon—but do come and see me again if you're still worried.'

The door opened abruptly and Neil stood on the threshold. His face was stony, his eyes like blue ice, then he noticed the patient and his stiffness noticeably eased. He held the door open for her, and she, poor woman, sensing the sudden charge of tension that had arisen, scuttled out.

Lesley rose to her feet and they faced each other across the desk. The silence was tangible like an ominous presence, then Lesley broke the spell.

'You've seen Chris?'

'I have, and I've also read Vita's letter. I have only one thing to say to you, Dr Colman—the next time you decide to play God please check your facts first!'

She winced at the tone of his voice.

'Would you believe me if I told you how very sorry I am?'

His smile was more like a sneer.

'The low opinion you have of me doesn't worry me one bloody damn, but I'll never forgive you for what you've done to Fran!'

He turned to stalk out, but she dashed round the desk and gripped him by his arm. 'You can't condemn me out of hand like that, you must let me defend myself! I acted as I did for Fran—I swear I was only thinking of Fran —and—and—' Oh, why not make a clean breast of it—she'd be out of Trevaise and away from them all soon. 'And I was thinking of your baby too. I couldn't bear the thought of it being destroyed.'

A curious gleam flickered in and out of his eyes and she thought she detected a slight softening of expression, but his voice was just as harsh when he said, 'And of course you were ready to believe it *was* my baby?'

There was no answer to that. Neil gave her one last unfathomable look and went out. Wearily she went back to her chair and slumped forward on her desk, her head in her arms. She was still in the same attitude when Miss Pearson looked in.

'Oh, sorry, Dr Colman, I didn't mean to intrude.' Then as Lesley looked up, 'Are you all right?'

'Just a little tired, that's all,' Lesley sighed.

'I wouldn't have bothered you, but it's old Mr Green—he's run a fish-hook into his finger. I told him both Dr Rodway and Dr Watling were out, so he said he'd see you.'

With some effort Lesley resurrected her sense of humour. 'Not willingly, I bet!'

Miss Pearson reddened but smiled. 'No, not exactly. He said something like—"Needs must when the devil drives". Shall I send him in?'

Lesley straightened her back. 'Miss Pearson, I've been indulging in a bout of self-pity—old Mr Green is just the person to chivvy me out of it. Yes, send him in.'

After Mr Green had gone, his opinion of female doctors undergoing a quick change, Lesley sat on waiting for Chris. He came straight to her room as soon as he got back, looking unusually buoyant for a man who had gone through a traumatic interview with his wife.

'How's Fran?' Lesley asked anxiously.

'Fine—fine. We worried for nothing. She took the news in her stride.'

Lesley couldn't believe this, and her anxiety increased.

'Don't you think that's odd? To be suddenly faced with the news that she isn't going to have Vita's baby after all? I thought she would be hysterical, it would have been more in keeping. Perhaps she's bottling it all up—perhaps she'll do something desperate—'

Chris gave an exasperated sigh. For the first time since knowing him he showed impatience.

'It's you who's hysterical. Don't you think I know my wife after all these years? She took the news extremely philosophically. She shrugged and said, "What is to be will be". Do you think I'd have come straight here from Polhearne if I was at all concerned about her? I'd have called in at the cottage first. You're overwrought. Get off home, you'll find her there with your lunch waiting for you.'

Lesley jog-trotted all the way to Cliff Cottage, still not convinced by Chris's easy assurance. She couldn't throw off a feeling of impending doom. She didn't believe that Fran had taken the disappointment so calmly. She was stunned perhaps, but simmering underneath, and heaven help them all when the lid blew off!

The cottage was empty. Lesley went from room to room, but there was no sign of Fran. Then in the kitchen she found a note taped to the door of the fridge.

> . . . Dear Lesley or Chris, whoever's in first, There's ham and salad in the fridge. I've gone to Pencade to take some things to old Nellie Briggs. Home by teatime.

An innocent enough message, almost identical with others Fran had left before, but to Lesley it suddenly had sinister undertones. Why Nellie Briggs—and why today of all days?

Her heart gave a sudden leap as words Fran had once uttered came back to mind: 'When anyone has been married for ten years and is beginning to get desperate —yes, they would try witchcraft.' And old Nellie was renowned for her magic potions—some noxious brews she made from herbs, and God knew the harm they could cause.

Lesley didn't stop to rationalise her thoughts, to tell herself that Fran was a doctor's wife and even desperation wouldn't drive her to such lengths. By now she was too desperate herself to think clearly. She took the short cut round the back of the cottage and on to the cliff road. The tide was full, filling the bay with an opalescent blueness so that she couldn't take the shorter route to Pencade along the beach. She had a three-mile walk ahead of her and then a long steep scramble down the cliff path.

She had gone little more than a mile when she heard a shattering noise of minor explosions and clattering metal behind her, then a car—or what had once been a car—drew up beside her. The driver, a long-haired youth with a wispy beard, grinned cheerfully. It was only young Steve Bourne, but to Lesley at that moment he was a knight in shining armour.

'Oh, Steve, am I pleased to see you! Can you give me a lift?'

'I'll do anything for you, Doctor—even risk your life in my jalopy! Hop in.'

Hopping in was easy—there were no doors.

'Steve, however did you get this licensed!' gasped Lesley.

'I didn't, but don't tell anyone. I'm taking it along to

the dump and 'oping to pick up something better.'

He couldn't possibly pick up anything worse, but Lesley wasn't worried, it was getting her that much quicker to Fran. She had got to know Steve very well since his mother's operation—Lesley asked after her now.

'She's getting on 'andsome—'opes to be walking without her stick soon. She still can't get down on her knees properly, though she 'as a good try. I scrub the floors in the meantime.' He looked sheepish as if it was unmanly admitting to domestic chores. His thoughtfulness was one of the things Lesley liked about him.

Fran's car came into sight, parked at the start of the cliff path. Steve pulled up with another series of explosions, scaring a hare out of its form and sending it streaking across the field.

''Ope I 'aven't shook your liver up too much, Doctor.' He gave her another grin in farewell and went off in a cloud of black smoke and a final retort from the exhaust.

The cliff path was more overgrown than in early summer, strands of bramble tore at Lesley's dress and snagged her tights, but she pushed on uncaring. Then she saw Fran—perched on a grassy knoll staring out at sea. She heard Lesley coming and turned to watch her. There was a look of serenity about her.

She patted the ground by her side. 'I was hoping you'd come when you read my note. You do look exhausted—come and sit down.'

Exhausted! Lesley felt as if she had been through a mangle, as she dropped down beside Fran and asked the question that had nagged her all the way there.

'Why have you been to see old Nellie Briggs?'

'I haven't been yet. I went to Roshaven first, then did

some shopping. I got as far as this and felt tired, so I thought I'd rest a while.'

Lesley went back over her trauma of the past few hours—the effect of Fran's note on her, the mad dash along the cliff path—and here she was, calmly and unconcernedly looking out at sea. Lesley could have strangled her!

'I thought you'd gone to old Nellie's for some of her home-made fertility pills,' she said bitterly. 'I've been through hell ever since I got your note.'

Fran looked as if she didn't know whether to laugh or cry. She put out a hand in a gesture of contrition.

'Don't scold, dear. I'm so happy—don't spoil this day for me. Lesley, I'm pregnant!'

Lesley abruptly came up to a sitting position, too startled to make comment.

Fran's eyes looked as if they had lamps shining behind them. 'I've suspected for some weeks now. I went to see Dr Bradley at Roshaven and swore him to secrecy just in case I was mistaken—I couldn't raise Chris's hopes and then dash them again. Today I called for the result of my pregnancy test, and it's positive. I've just been sitting here blissfully wallowing—looking around me with fresh eyes. Everything—everywhere has a kind of magic about it—in a way I'm scared I shall suddenly wake up and find it's all a dream.'

Lesley felt in a dreamlike trance herself. 'So that's why you took Vita's news so calmly—you were already sure you were pregnant! And I thought you'd gone to poor old Nellie for help—' Something seemed to stick in Lesley's throat. 'I'm sorry, Fran.'

'So you should be,' said Fran cheerfully. 'Shame on you, for thinking I would resort to witchcraft. Dr Bradley is a wise old chap—guess what he said? That I conceived because I was in a happy and contented frame of mind—that before I was too over-anxious. So you see I'm still indebted to Vita, and you too, my dear.'

'What would you have done if Vita's baby was still available for adoption?' asked Lesley.

'Had twins, of course, with a few months' difference in their age!' Fran laughed and got to her feet. She picked up the basket of provisions she had brought for Nellie Briggs. 'Are you rested?—come along then, a quick visit to old Nellie and then home to break the glad tidings to Chris!'

They found Nellie Briggs in a poor state. She had crawled to the palliasse she used as a bed and had collapsed there—she could have lain there helpless for some days; she was filthier than ever and her breathing harsh and laboured. Lesley knelt beside her and gave her a swift going-over. She felt her forehead, which was feverish, and percussed the thorax, then she turned her gently and percussed her side and back.

'Pneumonia and pleurisy too, I suspect,' she told Fran. 'We'll have to get her to hospital. Fran, will you go—you drive. I'll stay with her and do what I can.'

Lesley could do very little without medicines or medical aids. 'A doctor is only as good as his tools,' she told herself in a fit of despondency. She collected a bowl of water from the spring and wiped the old woman's face and forehead and made a cold compress for her brow. She cursed herself for not even having an aspirin on her—that could have helped to bring down the temperature.

Much later the sound of an approaching boat came like sweet music to her ears. Lesley realised it was the Trevaise lifeboat—a large inflatable dinghy with an outboard motor; of course, it would have been almost impossible to get poor old Nellie up the steep cliff path. She could see Neil in the bows and two men in oilskins—probably stretcher-bearers. The skipper manoeuvred the boat into shallow waters with an adroitness born of practice and Neil and the two men jumped out and splashed to the shore.

Lesley sank down on the sands and put her face in her hands. She was beyond exhaustion—she could feel nothing but relief that someone else could now take over responsibility.

Once his patient was safely in the boat Neil came over to her. 'Chris will be coming for you—do you mind waiting on? There's no room in the boat.'

'I don't mind,' she said wearily.

She felt the pressure of his hand on her shoulder. 'You've done a good job, Lesley. You and Fran between you, you've saved old Nellie's life.'

She watched him go off through a blur of tears—tears she was too weak to hold back. Tears of lassitude and relief and something else besides—gratitude because he had spoken to her so tenderly.

Nellie's rescue got front-page coverage in the local newspaper. Fran was credited with second sight because she had had the compulsion to visit the old recluse on that particular day, while Lesley was described as 'our brilliant and very popular temporary GP'. She couldn't raise a smile when she read that, though tears came readily when the tributes began to come in from some of her patients. Posies of cottage-garden flowers, home-made cakes, a dish of clotted cream, several mackerel—and one luxury she could well have done without—a lobster, still alive and active.

The time came to start making her goodbyes. One warm Saturday in September when the heather on the moors looked like a purple mantle she called at High Moors to see Mrs Fiske. Chris drove her there as he had a patient to visit in the vicinity, and would call back for her later. But Mrs Fiske had left for a holiday in Scotland and Colin was preparing for his trip to New York and his second exhibition there.

'When I first planned this I hoped you would be accompanying me,' he said, but in such a way she couldn't take him seriously.

'I've come to say goodbye—' she began.

He gave her a half-humorous, half-mocking look. 'So you're running away after all. I thought perhaps you would have changed your mind.'

'I'm not running away! You know my contract has expired—'

He interrupted with a mirthless laugh. 'Oh yes, you are running away—you're running from Neil Rodway, because you love him. Do you think I'm blind? You're a pair of stiff-necked idiots—and I don't see why I should help you, but I will.' He took a letter from his pocket. 'Would you deliver this to Rodway for me—it's only a receipt, but it would save me the bother of posting it.'

Nonplussed, Lesley took the letter and put it in her handbag. Why should Colin be sending Neil a receipt? They must have been in touch—but why?

Colin watched her with a wry expression. 'I can tell what you're thinking—yes, the cold war is over. He's even offered to fix my ankle for me—but I don't feel that beholden, not yet, anyway. Goodbye, Lesley—and good luck for your future.'

He took her by surprise and kissed her—fiercely on her lips. Quickly she drew back, and he gave one of his characteristic shrugs. 'No, you could never have loved me—you're a one-man girl, Lesley. Lucky chap—I only hope he's worthy of you!'

Chris was waiting in the drive, his calls were completed and he was free to take her back to Trevaise. He looked at her and asked, 'What's given you that high colour? Old Lady Fiske in one of her moods?'

'Actually she wasn't there, but I saw Colin. He gave me this for Neil—said it was a receipt.'

Lesley expected Chris to show surprise, but he just said, 'Oh yes.' He backed down the drive, then turned into the Trevaise road. Presently he began to sing; he was tone-deaf, but that didn't deter him. Lesley gritted her teeth and endured—after all, one had to make allowances for a father-to-be!

Chris followed her into Carn House and along the hall to the kitchen where Mrs Hatchet was to be found any time of day. She was just putting some scones in the oven, and her face lit up when she saw them.

'You've just called at the right time for a cup of tea,' she said, taking cups and saucers from the dresser.

But Lesley was on edge to deliver the letter and get away. She had no wish to meet Neil face to face on his home ground—even at the surgery she avoided him as much as possible. Since the rescue of Nellie Briggs and the news of Fran's pregnancy his antipathy towards her had faded away, but in its place had grown something just as disturbing, an excessive politeness which unnerved her to the point of awkwardness. They could no longer speak naturally to one another.

'Dr Rodway has gone out for a sail,' said Mrs Hatchet, taking cream from the fridge and jam from the larder in almost simultaneous movements. 'You *can* stay for tea?' as Lesley still hovered in the doorway.

Lesley had no intention of staying, she wouldn't feel

safe until she was clear of Carn House. She made some halting excuses and said she had only called to leave a letter for Neil.

'Well, I want some tea,' said Chris. She had never known him to be so aggravating, she couldn't understand why he hadn't waited for her in the car. She had said she'd only be a minute.

Mrs Hatchet said, 'Could you leave the letter in his study, Doctor—it will save my poor feet.'

This was the first Lesley had heard of Mrs Hatchet's poor feet. She went off to the study and to her annoyance Chris followed.

The door was ajar as usual—it was only ever shut when Neil was working in there. He had been working—writing letters; paper and envelopes were still lying about. Lesley put the letter on the desk where it would be noticed and turned to go again—then she saw Chris standing staring up at the portrait of Neil's grandmother which hung over the mantelpiece. But it couldn't be Neil's grandmother—Lesley could see *that* portrait from where she stood hanging on the opposite wall. Why had it been moved?

And Chris was wearing such a smug, self-satisfied expression. She had a sudden premonition and hurried across the room. Yes, it was the painting of herself—'The Girl with Daffodils'.

'I don't understand—' she faltered. She turned on Chris accusingly. 'You knew about this!'

'Yes, I knew.'

'And Mrs Hatchet knew!'

'Of course—why else did she send you along here, the crafty old bird?'

'I don't understand,' Lesley repeated in bewilderment. She looked at the painting again. 'Why should

Neil buy it? He didn't even go and see it when it was on exhibition.'

'Oh yes, he did—every day—and badgered Bucknall until he sold it to them. It looks very well here, don't you think—lights this old room up.'

It did have the effect of a pool of sunshine—and strange, Lesley thought—the painted eyes no longer looked sad, only wistful.

'I wonder why he bought it,' she said, voicing her thoughts aloud. She heard Chris shift his feet. Suddenly she felt the need to confide her pent-up longings, the dreams that would never be, and who better than to dear, kind, reliable Chris? 'Oh, Chris, if I could only believe he wanted the portrait because of me—but I know that isn't so. I suppose he bought it as an investment—Colin will be famous one day—but I wish—Oh, how I wish he'd bought it because it means something to him—that *I* mean something. But he'll let me go and I shall never know what he really thought of me.'

'You could always ask him.' But it wasn't Chris speaking—it was someone with a rich deep voice that froze the blood in her veins. She made a dash for the door, but he held her so fast she couldn't move, though she struggled, pushing against his shoulders with the palms of her hands. Tears of frustration and hurt pride filled her eyes.

'Go on, laugh,' she said bitterly at last.

'And why should I laugh?'

'Because now you know you can add me to your list of conquests—Dorinda and Vita and Moira and all the others—' she choked back fresh tears.

Neil put his hands either side of her face and wiped her eyes with a slow tender movement of his thumbs. Then he kissed them, and then her mouth—gently at first, then more hungrily as his passion kindled. Lesley tried to resist him, but the will-power wasn't there, and surrender was sweet when she knew as she did now, that he loved her in return.

'You sneaked in behind me,' she said when his hold lessened and she was able to look up at him, not accusingly, just with loving fervour.

'I saw Chris standing here with such a fatuous look on his face and motioned him out,' Neil explained.

'And Mrs Hatchet said you'd gone for a sail!'

'Mrs H is an angel in disguise. She knew I'd only gone to the post—she wanted me to catch you here.'

'Why didn't you tell me about the portrait?' demanded Lesley.

'I intended to give you a farewell party, and you would have seen it then.'

She traced the outline of his lips with her finger. 'I don't understand—you would have let me go from here without telling me how you felt?'

'I wasn't to know how *you* felt—I hadn't acted very kindly at times—I was an absolute boor at the interview. I said you would be a disruptive influence in the practice—what I meant was that you'd have a disruptive effect on me. I felt it in my bones—and good Lord, how right I was!' He placed his hands on her shoulders and stared hungrily into her eyes. 'The first time I realised how much I loved you was just before you left here to live at Cliff Cottage. I'd been to the Club and met Dorinda there and she walked back with me—she was staying with friends nearby, it was shortly after her husband had left for Nigeria. It was a moonlight night and she got rather amorous. I nearly succumbed to her very overt invitation, then I happened to see you outlined in your window. The moonlight gave you a misty effect and you looked like a Botticelli painting. Oh, Jane, my precious Jane—you bowled me over!'

She laughed shakily. 'I haven't been called Jane for years.'

'I shall call you nothing else. Lesley isn't feminine enough for you.' Neil led her to the sofa, sat down and pulled her down next to him. She remembered that once he had not thought her feminine enough—but that was all in the past. Only the future mattered now. 'And when will you marry me, my Jane? Don't keep me waiting too long!'

It couldn't be before October if it was to be a white wedding with Jan as bridesmaid, and they both wanted that. 'And for our honeymoon we'll go sailing off in *Seawife*—perhaps to the Scillies.'

Lesley snuggled closer against him—she couldn't believe that just making plans could bring such happiness.

'There's just one thing bothers me,' he said. 'Asking you to give up your career. You would have made a good surgeon.'

She looked at him with all the wisdom of a woman who loves and is loved in return.

'I'm not giving up my career—I'm expanding it. I shall be a wife as well as a doctor.'

Neil drew her closer with a sudden urgency. 'Wife—my wife,' he said before he kissed her. 'That sounds to me the sweetest word in the world.'

In the kitchen Chris helped himself to another scone. He had no more calls to make that afternoon, he was well content to sit and watch Mrs Hatchet as she rummaged in the dresser drawer.

'Lost something, Mrs H?'

'I've just found it—my grandmother's recipe for a wedding cake. I have a feeling I shall need it!'